DIFFICULT YEARS
on
JOHNSONS FARM

By
ARTHUR BATTELLE

The fourth COUNTRY LOVE story

DIFFICULT YEARS
On
JOHNSONS FARM

Book four in the "COUNTRY LOVE series

First published March 2000

Copyright Arthur Battelle

A catalogue record for this book is available from the British Library

ISBN 0-9530782-6-4

Published by

TRACPREZ PUBLICATIONS c/o
Old Twenty Parts Company,
Cavendish Bridge,
Shardlow,
Derby DE72-2HL

DIFFICULT YEARS
on
JOHNSONS FARM

The fourth story in the COUNTRY LOVE series, tells of the relief after the Great War finished. How Johnsons farm somehow survives the bad times of the 1920's and early1930's, things gradually improve. Then comes the Second World War, the farm has better days but is influenced by the nearby American Air force Base. How the family grows, the success of the Garage, how one member of the family leaves England for ever.

OTHER BOOKS IN THE

COUNTRY LOVE SERIES

Book one   Country Love
Book two   Johnsons Farm
Book three Johnsons Farm
                    At War

OBTAINABLE FROM

TRACPREZ PUBLICATIONS
c/o OLD TWENTY PARTS COMPANY
CAVENDISH BRIDGE,
SHARDLOW,
DERBY DE72- 2HL

Or any good agricultural book stockist

DIFFICULT YEARS FOR JOHNSONS FARM

Joe Johnson walked slowly across the home field in the direction of the spinney where Ted Rudge, Lord Jensen's head gamekeeper, raised most of the pheasants that were intended to provide His Lordships shooting party with most of their sport. It was July 1919, The Great War had been over for more than seven months and things were gradually returning to, what most people regarded as normal. This included renewing the autumn shoots that were such a feature of pre war life, this years shoots would be the first to be held on Jensen Estate since the war began and were keenly looked forward to by His lordship.

The spinney towards which Joe had been walking was in fact much more of a wood, it covered thirty five acres and was partly owned by Johnsons Farm and partly by Jensen Estates, Ted Rudge reared pheasants in both parts of the spinney and Johnsons Farm, in return were able to take fencing materials and firewood from all of the spinney.

Joe was walking towards the spinney, situated on high ground, not exactly a hill but offering a good view over most of the arable land farmed by Johnsons farm. Joe's intention was to look over these fields to form some sort of an idea how the corn crops were ripening, the harvest seemed likely to be early, as Joe looked over the fields he could see two fields of winter wheat that he felt might soon be ready to cut. Joe leaned on the gate separating home field from the next grass field, he cast his eye over the dairy herd gently grazing at the lower end of the second grass field and his thoughts strayed over the last few hectic years. The expansion of Johnsons Farm by taking over a run down neighbouring farm, the arrival of a Ford Lorry to replace the horse and trap for delivering the milk, to both the station and Johnsons Farm Dairy in the neighbouring town of Little Staunton. Joe also recalled how he had proposed that Johnsons Farm should buy the local garage, destined to close due to lack of new vehicles to sell, but Joe had realised how valuable the Ford franchise might be after the war was over, so they had purchased it and managed to keep it going over the war years.

Joe also recalled, with a smile, how the three children of Jane, his Wife and himself, had worked through the war, Jenny the eldest with the forces in France, where she had met a local boy from Jensen Village, who had later been killed, leaving Jenny desolate. But now she had an understanding with one of the patients she had helped to nurse in the French hospital, Joe also thought of his second child, Gil who had worked throughout the war with Frank Simpson on a threshing machine. Then of course Joe's youngest and only son Tom, who had driven one of the two Mogul tractors that had arrived on Johnsons Farm, the second being driven by Merri, daughter of the Manager of Johnsons Farm Dairies. Joe smiled to himself recalling how Frank and Gil, Tom and Merri, had decided to marry as soon as the war was over.

Turning back to November 1918, Merri and Gil, always good friends and confidants had decided they must marry soon. The pressures of war had eased and both girls had been rather carried away with loving feelings for their partners and were now trying, with little success, to hold a prudent and careful grip on their passionate actions. As Merri told Gil, it was only a matter of time before one or the other, either miscalculated or lost control at a vital time, so they both decided they must marry soon. All the families agreed and were relieved at that decision, so a joint wedding was planned, this was to take place during January 1919. All these 'shenanigans', as Joe called them amused him, he told Jane 'perhaps we should stop breeding cattle and start a baby farm'. Jane wanted to know if he was looking forward to becoming a grandparent, Ma. Jane's mother, offered her help, telling them both she was an experienced and happy Grandmother. They all became serious when Ma. told them how happy she would be to see another son for Johnsons Farm and how happy she knew her own Tom, now dead over twenty years, would have been to see a new son to succeed to the farm when the time came. Jane said how proud she was of the younger generation, how they had conducted themselves over the wartime years, even Jenny who was now flagrantly defying all convention, but could look back over the wartime years with pride. Ma. remarked that a lot of credit could be put down to the open and sensible way Jane and Joe had brought the children up.

Lord Jensen, partly due to his damaged leg and partly because he hoped to help influence the peace, by taking his seat in the House of Lords, was now released from the army and would probably be demobilised in the near future. The position of Rob, Jenny's boy friend, was very similar, but he still held his position in the army. The end of his service came unexpectedly, early in December Rob picked up a heavy cold, he knew it was serious for him due to the wartime damage to his lung. He used the inhaler solution Joe had provided for him to help and on the Friday he managed to drive his car home.

A message to Jenny brought her post haste with more inhaler from Joe, who now took over the lorry deliveries that Jenny normally did. On Saturday the doctor came and told them Rob had bronchitis, it would not normally be too serious, but with his lung problems from the wartime gas he must stay in the house, keep warm and rest in bed for a week. The doctor expressed an opinion that for a year or

3

two, at least, Rob must be very careful of the damp English winters, keeping well wrapped up and perhaps should think of a few weeks each winter being spent in a warmer and drier climate.

A medical note on this diagnosis was sent to Rob's regiment, along with a request for a discharge and an enquiry about an invalidity pension. Jenny spent the weekend with him and left for home on the Monday morning, later she took over the lorry again, but spent a deal of money on the telephone to Rob's home. The second week in December two more Fordson Tractors were delivered to the garage, one was on order, so that left one spare, Johnsons Farm decided to buy it, the old Mogul's had done a considerable amount of work and were now quite old. Merri was sent off to plough one of the easier and drier fields, with this new tractor to familiarise herself with it, ready to demonstrate other tractors to prospective customers for the garage when supplies became freely available.

Tom and Joe were regular visitors to the field, giving advice and congratulations, on how well Merri was working the new tractor. With the field just one day from completion, they held one of their regular evening meetings in the farm office, the object of this was to decide on the farms future tractor drivers. Joe told them now was the time to sell three more horses, leaving only two on the farm. This meant that one of the horsemen must become a tractor driver, Joe thought they should train both horsemen if the weather stayed good enough for them to keep ploughing, using the one Fordson tractor they had, Joe did not believe it was sensible to train anyone to drive the old Mogul tractors which were now likely to be retired.

Billy was the first of the men to start training, Tom and Merri set up a new field and were surprised how quickly Billy picked up the skills needed. During the afternoon Tom and Merri left Billy on his own, but one of them, usually Merri, returned about every hour, this procedure was repeated with Harry and within two weeks both men were mastering the skills required. One evening Gil and Merri joined together in Gil's room to discuss their joint wedding, each assuring the other that they were agreeable to have a double wedding. Both girls decided the reception should be held in Jensen Village Hall, also agreeing that the best kept secret of any wedding, the brides dress, had to be a joint decision, partly to avoid a clash of styles and partly to enable matching bouquets to set off the occasion with style. Having agreed on their thoughts, they decided the mothers could now be consulted, the next meeting to include all four mothers. Now Merri told Gil, ' one thing we must take into consideration is what date is the wedding to be', 'I thought we said the end of January ', Gil told her. 'We must be much more accurate than that Merri said', pointing out to Gil that the date was very important, unless they decided it did not matter if one, or both conceived a baby during their honeymoon. ' Oh, I see what you mean', Gil told her, as they calculated dates it became obvious they would not have to consider any problems if the wedding was arranged for January 18th, so that was the date they fixed.

The meeting with the mothers established that date, so the young couples visited the Rev. James to make arrangements for the wedding, they all knew he was shortly to retire, now the war was over, and a new vicar had been selected. The Rev. was so pleased to hear their news and told them it would be a very joyous occasion for him, reminding them he had known them all their lives and would be so happy to marry them as his final celebration in Jensen parish church, you know he told them,' a retiring vicar just dreads having to conduct a funeral as his last duty, but a double wedding that is indeed a celebration'. It then transpired that the date they had chosen was to be the date of the new vicars induction, but the Rev. James said he could marry them the week before and hoped that would be acceptable. Later Gil and Merri sat in Gil's room looking at the calendar, Merri just knew they must have the Rev. James to marry them, telling Gil they would just have to be careful with their lovemaking for the first few nights, hopefully all would go well, but in any case she felt one or perhaps both of them, would fall for a baby within a couple of months anyway.

Jenny spent a lot of time with Rob, he had now recovered a little, but as the doctor told him, he would always have problems with colds and influenza and must be very careful. The Army had requested his attendance before a medical board on January the fifth, so Jenny and Rob did not take part in Johnsons Farm New Year Dinner for the staff, which again was to be held in the village hall. All the staff were present, Bessie and Bob, who was on leave were invited, everyone marvelling at the spread put on by Johnsons Farm and congratulating Ma, who was considered the organiser of a great event.

Rob had been driven to appear before the medical board by Jenny, their wedding had been delayed due to Robs health, but now he was improving they had, much to parents disgust, decided on a civil ceremony at Staunton Register Office on January 7th. not wishing to conflict with the double wedding at Jensen. It was now accepted by both Robs Mother and Jane that they were married in all but name, Jenny now allowing Rob to use a protector so she did not conceive, but making him aware that on their honeymoon, these were banned. For some reason, maybe shyness or not wishing to make herself appear "cheap", Jenny had not mentioned the protectors to Gil, nor had

Jane or Meg, both believing it was better for young wives to enjoy a natural marriage, at least until the first baby came along.

With the tractors not now needing Merri, she was taking Jenny's place on the lorry, Tom was ploughing full time with the Mogul and either Billy or Harry accompanying him with the Fordson. Jensen Estates were now using the new Fordson supplied by the Garage, as was Rory Deane on Spinney Farm, Rory driving it himself. So now Johnsons Farm did not expect to work for either of those two farms again with their tractors. The wedding plans were going apace, dresses bought, new clothes for the honeymoon and now it was time to visit Jensen with Rob and Jenny for their wedding. A safe dignified ceremony and a return to Johnsons Farm for a typical Johnsons Farm meal, but now the dining room was polished and set out with so much food and of course the inevitable tea pot, family size. They sat down on chairs that the younger generation and that included Jane and Joe, could not remember last being used. It was a long meal but a happy one, much banter about marriage, Jenny now able to allow herself a longing for Rob that somehow she had not noticed before.

The four who were now on the threshold of marriage looked longingly at Jenny and Rob sitting at the head of the polished table, but realising that next week they would be in this position, it was a tantalising prospect. Joe finally stood and with Champagne offered a toast to Jenny and Rob, Andrew, Rob's brother made a short speech to which Rob responded, it was all very friendly and low key. Jane drove the newly weds to the station on the first stage of their honeymoon, which was to be spent in Cornwall. A hotel had been recommenced where, at least a little winter sunshine may be expected, the journey was to be broken in London at a rather expensive hotel, but it was not until they arrived in Cornwall that Jenny settled to her new life. The hotel was high, overlooking the sea and of course, not full, Rob and Jenny had a room with a sea view, a fire when required, a warm sunlounge for afternoon tea and a good dining room. The cliff top paths offered exercise and sea air, good for Rob's lung, probably much better for him was Jenny, they spent the first day exploring, three days later Rob could walk, steadily it was true, without the breathless coughing that had troubled him at home.

Now of course his demands on Jenny began to increase, they were met enthusiastically, until one day he asked if he should now use the protectors he had with him, Rob realising the time for caution was now approaching, Jenny laughed, you are too late, you should have used them three days ago, but I would never have let you.

Farmwork at Jensen was progressing as usual, but not, it must be said, with the concentration from Tom and Merri that it normally received, whilst Frank was being pressed by his Mother to buy clothes and the many things a bridegroom should pack for his honeymoon, Frank was suffering stoically. Merri was now in a haze of new clothes, cases, weddings and various arrangements until she lost count of the number of visits to shops she had made with Gil. usually accompanied by their mothers. Gil had often heard her mother refer to the hotel in Yarmouth where she spent her short honeymoon, Gil suggested that they spend their joint honeymoon at the same hotel, luckily it had not been damaged during the war and was pleased to accept their booking, it sounded wonderful when the booking was confirmed for Mr. and Mrs. Simpson and Mr. and Mrs Johnson.

The first week of January, although cold was dry and some spring work had already started, the Fordson had been well serviced and now was finishing the winter ploughing, Joe estimated it had about three weeks work left to do. Tom had returned to the Mogul and was teaching Billy to use it, in case it was needed to do some harrowing or top cultivating before Tom returned from his honeymoon. No more Fordson tractors had arrived and none were expected before the end of April, Joe and Tom were hoping that one might come so the grass and corn cutting could be done with two Fordson tractors which would both travel at the same speed, the old Mogul was both slower and much more cumbersome.

The day of the wedding eventually, with much impatient waiting, arrived, everything was in turmoil, the caterers had set out the village hall early, they would move in to make the final settings later. Tessa, Merri's mother, Ellenor, Franks mother and Jane had spent hours working out place settings, a double wedding seemed four times more complicated than a single one. The two families had, on the Friday evening gone through a form of rehearsal, but with other things on their minds and with the pressures of preparation resting on them, it is doubtful if the rehearsal's helped. The ceremony was scheduled for 11.30am, and a full hour before that the Johnson farm horse yard was full of horses and traps and motor cars, the village street was filling with vehicles as was the spare ground around the village hall. It would be wonderful to say the sun shone, but the day was cloudy with a cold wind, but at least it was dry, at eleven o'clock the street and the drive leading to the church was full of family parties walking to the wedding.

Tom had asked his friend John Deane to stand with him and Bill was to lead his daughter, Merri, down the isle. Frank had an ex school friend and Joe was to escort Gil to the alter, new and modern fashions were rife.

The Reverend James rose to the event, the church shone and although it was mid winter, flowers were placed in

9

strategic places to add brightness. Of course photographs were now an important part of any wedding, some outside the church for each couple and a rather wonderful one showing the two newly wed couples walking together the few yards to the village hall, with the church showing in the background. The reception and wedding breakfast were well conducted, but of course, at this event there were two lots of speeches to both bore and amuse. Many old jokes about being sure to take the correct bride to bed and other rather ancient cracks, all taken in good part with laughter to brighten the occasion. Eventually the cake was cut and later the two newly married couples were driven to Johnsons farm to change for their journey to a new life.

It was history repeating itself, just as Jane and Joe had left Little Staunton station over twenty years ago now two of their children were undertaking the same journey, what might the result be. There was still need for a male heir for the farm, it was no longer Jane and Joe who had this responsibility, they had completed their part of the dynasty, now Tom and his wife Merri must take over, how would they fare in undertaking this responsibility. How would Gil achieve her responsibility to provide a heir for the Simpson family, also there was a strong possibility that Jenny might soon provide a son for the Graham farm, so as 1919 began the next generation was almost within sight.

The Hotel in Great Yarmouth was warm and inviting after the sleet swept promenade, the two couples were welcomed and taken to their rooms, the reception telling them that dinner would be served from seven o'clock, in about one hours time. Tom lay luxioriously on the bed watching Merri unpack their clothes, as she worked they talked of the wedding and how wonderful it was to be free of restrictions at last, well almost free Merri reminded him, intimating they must be careful! how far they allowed their feelings to carry them for at least a few days yet. Looking across the room at Merri, Tom realised she was clipping the empty case and storing it beside the wardrobe, with a smile on his face he told her to walk over to him, he needed a cuddle, just before dinner. Merri turned to the bed and bent over Tom, kissing him fully on his lips, Tom pulled her to him and she half fell onto the bed, mind my dress Merri told him, I do not want it creased, well take it off she was told. A few seconds hesitation and Merri hung up the dress in the wardrobe, in the meantime Tom had taken off his new trousers and returned to the bed, Merri joined him and they spent a glorious few minutes of loving freedom together. There was no shyness between them, they had worked together throughout the war on the tractors and were aware of one anothers bodies, they had to react to the calls of nature and even on some occasions they had, after a really soaking morning at work, changed into dry clothes together when the rain had stopped, but this was different now married and in a warm room, they had never experienced a situation like this before. After some time Tom placed his hand on Merri's breast, she did not object, just kissed him again and sighed, eventually she moved her hand inside the elastic of Tom's underpants and held one of his buttocks, as they lay together Merri could feel the urgency of Tom but as he slipped his hand into her pants and started to take them off Merri told him he must stop. Explaining, what he already knew, that it was not the right time of the month to take a chance, she did not want to end as a pregnant mum from her honeymoon, although she might allow him to make love without restriction over the next month after their return home.

The next day, after a late breakfast they walked around the town to see what the winter shops had to offer, but it was bitterly cold, arriving back at the hotel they were pleased to find the rooms tidy, beds made and a fire burning in each room, just before lunch Frank suggested they should take a drink in the bar, the two men took a pint each and the girls a port and lemon, feeling much warmer now, they had a good lunch with a bottle of wine and decided to take another walk to prepare themselves for dinner. As Tom and Merri sat in their room by a nice warm fire, they looked out over a grey sea and could plainly see a miserable sleet blowing almost horizontally over the beach. Tom asked his wife whose idea it was to go out in such weather, suggesting they cancel the outing, telling Merri they had a telephone, why not use it to ring Gil and tell her they would meet in the sun lounge for afternoon tea at four pm. Merri enquired what he had in mind for the afternoon, Tom, Quizzically raising an eyebrow, suggested perhaps they could play cards. Tom was reminded that was all they should do for the next few days, Merri was still concerned about having a baby too soon, as Tom listened to her he suggested perhaps he should try and persuade her to forget babies and concentrate on him. Merri laughing, told him that might be easy for him to do, but he had better not try, as they sat laughing together the telephone rang, as one they said Gil, "leave it to me" Merri told him, lifting the receiver Merri paused for a moment with it in mid air and with a faltering voice said Tom let me reach it properly, putting it closer to her ear she heard Gil say " is that you Merri, you sound different", "Oh yes it is me, what do you want", " Frank and I think it is too cold to walk, what do you think". Before answering Merri turned away from the phone saying " Tom behave yourself", Gil soon picked up that Merri was perhaps involved with Tom in some way, this was reinforced when Merri said " Tom stop that you will break the elastic"," hey Merri what are you doing", Gil almost shouted, " not much, but Tom is trying hard", Merri told her. " Well remember the date Merri was warned", " I had almost forgotten when you called", Merri said, then " wait Tom","Merri be careful ", Gil warned, " Oh it's all right Tom just loves to fool around, Tom behave yourself", then to Gil "shall we meet for afternoon tea at four o'clock, and Gil just ask Frank to undo the buttons down the back of your frock, you never know where that may lead, bye then sweetie be careful".

As Merri replaced the telephone they both burst out laughing, " I bet you got Gil worried now, but it was a good idea to tell her to ask Frank to help her out of her frock, obviously I can learn from you, stand up and I will help you off with yours". Tom walked to the door and turned the key, coming back with a coat hanger in his hand, Merri watched him without moving, putting the coat hanger on the bed Tom came to Merri, carefully kissing her and at the same time easing her out of the chair until their lips met, almost level, he put his arms around her as Merri placed hers around his neck. Tom broke away enough to speak, telling Merri he never knew how devious she could be, how he could just see his sister shocked and yet jealous of Merri, lying on the bed with her husband. " You never know Tom maybe Gil is ahead of us now, I still have my dress on",

Tom gently untwined her arms from around his neck, as Merri stood demurely in front of him Tom unfastened the buttons between her breasts and down to her waistline, he then gently slipped the dress off her shoulders being sure to take the straps of her underskirt with it. Slowly lifting her arms and carefully bending each one in turn, Tom pulled the dress sleeves clear, allowing the dress and underskirt to slide down to the floor. Merri stepped clear, Tom kissed her again, then feeling a rising excitement in her he moved Merri to the bed, sitting her on the side, Tom rolled down her stockings, he picked up the clothes from the floor hanging them in the wardrobe. Turning towards Merri again, he was surprised to see she had taken off the remaining top garments and sat looking at him with shining eyes, two small but perfectly formed breasts and a smile on her lips. " I thought we were not taking chances to-day", Tom told her, " Oh Tom, trying to set Gil up seems to have set me up even more, but you are right, we must not take a chance on me being caught with a baby for at least another day, better still two days. Tom enquired "what about my sister, you may have a responsible husband who will not go too far with you, but what will Frank do", "Tom darling that is for Gil to decide, in two days we can play, but Gil is only just entering a time when she must act responsibly.

As Tom sat by Merri she held him tight, kissing him with some passion, as he returned her kiss, Merri pulled him so gently backwards, until they lay side by side, their lips still in contact. Eventually they broke away smiling at one another, then Merri showed Tom a red mark on her thigh, complaining that his belt buckle was making her leg sore, Telling Merri he was so sorry and would take it off, " the buttons on your trousers are almost as bad, so take them off as well , in any case we do not want them creased". Tom sat up and took off his trousers and underpants, returning to the bed he placed his lips on hers and gently cupped her left breast, Merri slowly detached one arm from around Tom's neck, sliding her hand down his chest and stomach, Tom felt a surge of need as her hand found its target. The time passed as they lay together until, breaking away, Merri told him " we must stop, passion was going too far, the telephone has a lot to answer for". Tom remarked" how do you think Gil is faring", "never mind Gil, I am in serious trouble, it has never been so difficult to deny myself", Merri told him. " What about me sweetheart, I need

14

you more than I have ever done, is it really so dangerous to love one another today", "Oh I don't know, maybe not but how can I tell, if you need me so badly kiss me again, we might not get caught for a baby", "No Merri, no more kisses just lie together whilst we recover, turn over on your side and I will lie by you".

They lay quietly together, Tom with one arm round Merri, the other gently resting on her chest, Merri feeling the urgency in Tom, quietly held him, hoping the demanding spontaneous actions she could feel would soon subside. Some time later Merri turned towards him his need seemed, to her, greater than ever, Tom gently massaged first one breast then the other until the nipples were coloured and hard. He lifted himself to reach over and kiss each in turn, finally slipping his lips to her throat and then meeting her half open lips, as Merri placed one arm around his neck, Tom almost without thinking slipped his hand inside the elastic of her knickers and gently stroked the tight curly hair he knew was there.

That seemed to be the catalyst, Merri slowly moved his head away from her lips, Tom could see two large shining eyes staring at him, " Quick take off my pants, I must love you now", Merri told him. Steady, Tom told her we agreed no babies, Tom kissed her " think it out", he told her, " I have and so have you, so stop holding back, you want it as bad as I do". Merri eased up and Tom slid off her honeymoon pants, specially made as the work ones were, but these in satin and not cotton. As tom gently eased himself over Merri he asked if she really knew what they were doing, no and I don't care was her reply, very soon Tom was sliding inside Merri, she was totally relaxed and nature just took its course for the next hour which simply disappeared as if it were but five minutes. Afterwards they lay together having so much enjoyed the torrent of release

15

they had both experienced, there was no worry now, it was too late for that, just a wonderful memory of love and passion. Tom lay by Merri, who all at once giggled, " better than by the tractor eh", " are you mad at me", Tom enquired, " not even with myself, how wonderful to be married", Merri told him. Laughing Tom enquired how many children they might have, " probably two", was the reply, "one every year if we behave like to-day" Merri was told, "but Tom it will be different when we are at home".

In the sun lounge they sat together with a pot of tea, Gil suggested Merri go with her to look at the shop counter in the entrance hall, walking out together, away from the men Gil asked what Merri was doing when Gil spoke to her on the telephone. Actually nothing Merri told her, "I was just trying to make you think we were in bed","well you certainly did so, that remark about the buttons on my dress really got us going, we have been in bed until a short time ago". "Gil that must have been lovely", "yes but it will be so difficult to stop now for the rest of our holiday, and I really should be careful", Merri told Gil not to be silly why does it matter.

Gil soon reminded Merri about not being caught with a baby on their honeymoon, the laugh is on me Merri told her "after trying to set you off this afternoon, I found that it was impossible to stop, I had stirred up feelings I never knew I had, so it is possible you see before you a new mum". Gil wanted to know if it really was so difficult to say no, " impossible" Merri told her, " just let it happen, we can work something out, perhaps after the first baby arrives.

The week passed quickly, a haze of shopping, walking, careless loving and an exchange of experiences between the girls just made them more demanding of their husbands. Tom and frank had soon lost interest in being careful with their new wives and were more than ready to meet every new desire that the girls offered. The night

16

before they left for home they all met in Gil and Frank's room, talking over their weeks honeymoon all agreed how wonderful it had been, but both Gil and Merri decided they were almost certainly having babies, all four agreed that in spite of their intentions not to be caught for a baby on honeymoon, they had almost certainly failed and were now wondering what the future might hold.

It was now almost seven months since the four had shared the January honeymoon and Merri was now a well made pregnant wife, Gil was in the same happy state, but had experienced much morning sickness, Merri had not had that problem, both were however, happy and looking forward to their babies. Frank's mother Ellenor, who had tried for so long to produce a brother or sister for Frank, was overjoyed when Gil told her she was having a baby, nothing was too much trouble and indeed Gil was being regularly spoilt.

Tom was learning about farming and Johnsons farm in particular, Joe was a good teacher, Tom had worked the tractor for most of the war so needed no learning about arable farming, before that he had helped with the dairy herd. Now Tom and his Dad were almost inseparable, visiting markets and sales, planning the next years crop rotation and manuring schedules, mending gates, doors, windows and machinery. Joe was also working closely with Tom collecting the countryside bounty of herbs and roots for the natural medicines his Romany background had taught him. Tom was becoming fascinated with all this, especially the complexities of the farm and each day his interest grew, although he often secretly thought how difficult it would be to equal his fathers skill in so many things that Joe did.

Jane and Ma, worked in the kitchen during the harvest, both hay and corn, Johnsons farm kitchen had always provided field meals for the workers at this busy time, this was partly to ensure they ate well and became a team and it also saved many hours walking from field to cottage and back, particularly when the work was on the outlying parts of the farm such as Riverside or Moorside farms. Jane was becoming more than ever concerned about her mother, although not an old lady, she was approaching her sixty-eighth year and was visibly slowing down from the sprightly middle aged lady of a few years ago. Ma. as everyone knew her, had married Tom Johnson in the 1860's and had delayed having a child until Jane came along after five years of marriage. When Johnsons farm had recovered from the very bad farming conditions it had to survive when Ma. was newly married.

She had often told the children that she had never been away from the farm since her marriage, except when she was needed to be with one of the village girls to help deliver a baby. Only then on very rare occasions had her voluntary midwife duties kept her away all night. All attempts to persuade Ma. to take a holiday had failed, she had repeatedly told them the only place she ever wanted to be was on Johnsons farm, her home. Joe and Jane had given up trying to persuade Ma. to rest, it was not in her nature to do so, but she must have been able to recognise her decreasing powers, because one day she had told Jane that although she had delivered Jane's children, Jane must now take over the new generation, although Ma. did insist that she must be present. Jane of course agreed, she had by now the skill to do so, acquired by the many births she had attended with Ma., her mother. Of course Jane told Ma. the youngsters may prefer to go to hospital for the birth, "Ah you are wrong, both girls have asked me if I will help them", Ma. told Jane. " Even Gil will come home when the time comes, Ellenor is in agreement, she has told Gil she has never delivered a baby.

What of Jenny, at this time her marriage to Rob Graham was also about to produce the next generation, married shortly before her sister Gil and Merri, Jenny was not certain when her baby was due. Jenny certainly seemed further advanced towards Motherhood than the other two wives, although only married shortly before them, Jenny made no secret of the fact that she had often slept with Rob before they were married, but had not intended to start a family until after the ceremony. Rob had access to the simple birth control protectors of that period and had regularly used them, neither Jenny or Rob would use the heavy, passion killing vulcanised rubber types of the time, latex protectors were not obtainable in those years. The preferred protectors were made from animal intestines, very light and reasonably pleasant to use, also fairly reliable.

During the war some army personnel had been introduced to these by the many girls who were to be found behind the lines in France, although their services were expensive, this meant it was usually only the officers who took advantage of these opportunities. Many of these personnel had, when they returned to England, left arrangements in France to have supplies of these protectors posted to them, thus they may say that a letter from France was expected, in other words a French letter.

Jenny and Rob had lately found a source for these protectors in England, indeed Meg who lived on Riverside farm producing pigs for Johnsons farm, had been producing them and using them for a number of years already. Meg had told no one about this because the basic intestine was part of the Johnsons farm pig, but recently she had confided in Jane that she both used and made them. However both Jane and Meg agreed it was better to allow both Gil and Merri to stay in ignorance of this availability until at least the first baby arrived. "Ah playing god again", Joe told Jane when he was told of this.

Visiting the doctor in Little Staunton at the beginning of August, Jenny had to accept that the baby might arrive about the end of that month. This left both herself and Rob thinking when she might have been caught without protection, they had certainly not intended this to happen, but as Jenny told Rob, at that time she had not bothered to remind him too keenly just when she thought he should be sure to take precautions.

Jenny and Rob were now part owners of Staunton Garage, Rob had bought twenty one per cent of the business from Ma. when he had married Jenny, jointly they had bought a house nearby and had set up home there, and now ran the garage together. Rob had only one good lung, the other had been damaged by shrapnel and gas during the war. Often he suffered during the winter with colds and bronchial complaints. Indeed the doctor had told him how lucky he had been top survive the terrible flu epidemic of 1918. Both Rob and Jenny were aware of this problem and that was the main reason Jenny had not wanted to delay having a family. Robs brother Andrew already thirty three years of age was totally dedicated to improving the pedigree dairy herd and stated he did not intend to marry, so the Graham farm seemed to be relying on Rob to provide a son to carry on the farm. Jenny of course being aware of this had hoped for a son as soon as possible so he could become established as a successor to Andrew and Rob, being educated in line with that ambition. Rob had once shocked Jenny by confiding in her that he believed his brother, hard working, well educated and smart, preferred the company of men to that of women.

There was much talk in the country, at that time, about the effect the aftermath of war was having on the families who had been overjoyed to have husbands and boy friends return from the fighting, the result could now be seen quite openly, as one wife after another started to experience an increase in the size of their waistline. In Jensen there were eight husbands returned during the period January to April, now there were six wives who were obviously growing larger by the day. Four village girls had married rather hurriedly, Just how nature was going to cope with the loss of millions of men, leaving a whole generation of women and girls without a man, had yet to be seen but no doubt mother nature would cope adequately.

The influence of Tom on Johnsons farm was beginning to show, Tom and his Dad had visited the newly reformed Agricultural Show after its wartime rest, there they had seen a horse rake to gather the remains of the hay or corn crops left in the field after the pickers had loaded the crop on to the harvest waggons. The rake was also used to drive across the swathes of hay, ready for carting, drawing three or four swathes into one, thus making the pickers job, never easy, but just a little bit easier. The main thing that Tom had suggested was to purchase an elevator, this was a large ramp with moveable tines driven by a small petrol engine. The harvest waggon was drawn up to its base and the load discharged, forkfull by forkfull, but always downwards, to be carried by the elevator up to the stack, however high it may be, thus even one of the farm women could unload the harvest waggons. The punishing heavy work of lifting the hay or grain upwards from the waggon to the stack was no more, the higher the stack the higher the elevator could be lifted by turning a handle at its side.

The purchase of the elevator meant the two Irishmen, who came every year to unload the harvest waggons, were no longer needed, but Joe, always looking to treat good workmen well, had intended to use the two for picking in the field. The problem was solved by the Jensen Estates farm employing them, so Johnsons farm, for the first time in many years, could harvest its crops with its own staff. The fact that the root harvest followed the hay and corn and no prisoner of war gangs were now available, might pose problems later in the autumn, but that was something both Tom and his Dad were aware of. The hay harvest had gone well, Merri still being able to drive an ageing "Boy" with the trap around the fields, taking drinks and meals to the workers, it was not expected that Merri would do this job in the corn harvest.

Having walked the fields and decided seventy five acres of winter grown wheat was almost ready for cutting, Joe talked to the family that evening in the office. The main subject was how to use the staff available to the best advantage, there were eight village women available when required, part of the agreement Joe had made many years ago, by guaranteeing at least one days work every week throughout the year, so long as they came for as long as the farm needed them at busy times. Six full time men, including Tom and Joe, Elizabeth Knowles, (Liz) from moorside farm and Jane her sister who could be called upon when wanted. June Arnold who now helped her mother in the dairy and Jacky Arnold who was now just beginning to work on the farm. The labour breakdown was difficult, Joe always loaded the waggons in the field, Bill and Walter, the German ex prisoner, picked the sheaves to the waggon. Jane had always ferried the loaded waggons to the stackyard and returned the empty waggons to the field. Jim Knowles unloaded the waggons on to the elevator and Billy Arnold with his son Jacky built the stack. The two Fordsons driven by Tom and Harry Down pulled the two corn binders, Janice seymour, not at this time needed to help her father Walter with the cows, rode binder for Tom whilst Harry had June Arnold riding binder for him. Two of the village women always helped milk, the other six formed two teams of people to set up stooks behind each binder, they often dropped behind if the cutting went well, but then the cutting teams always helped finish stooking before starting another field. Elizabeth Knowles was to do odd jobs and take the place of any lady who may not arrive for work. This only left the kitchen to be staffed, but of course there was a heavy demand for cool drinks and meals to meet, Ma. had always been in charge of the kitchen and Joe now asked her to take Jill Worsley, a workers wife, and Jane Knowles to work with her, he hoped Ma would now take the food to the workers using "Boy" and the trap.

What about me, asked Merri, I hope you will help in the kitchen and perhaps use your skills with Jill's two children, joe suggested, perhaps the experience will stand you in good stead. Of course Merri agreed, but Joe knew she was not happy, he suggested that perhaps they could persuade Jane Knowles to work as baby nurse after the harvest so Merri could, if she wished, return to driving the lorry full time. Oh yes Merri told them, that I would love and next harvest I want to drive one of the corn cutting tractors, that is a long time away yet, Joe told her, perhaps you will be having another baby by then, no chance Merri told Joe, looking at Tom, Merri told him to take note and behave himself.

Joe turned to Ma. do you agree with my way of organising the harvest and will you be happy to run around the fields with the meals, no Ma. told him, I shall not be happy but I know it is not possible for me to work as I would used to, so I will do as you ask. Tom are you satisfied with the way I have laid out our staff, yes Dad, you have done a good job, but it will cost a fortune in wages, it will be possible to pay those wages now, but if the price of crops go down, as I expect they will, can we go on like this.

The harvest went well, by the end of August the wheat stood in six large stacks, the oats and barley were being cut, twenty five acres of beans were beginning to turn from green to black, but Joe estimated another four weeks before they were ready for cutting. All at once the harvest was disrupted by a telephone call from Rob, Jenny was having the baby could Ma. and Jane go at once. Elizabeth was then put on delivering the loads to the stack and Jessie Knowles moved into the kitchen to help. The special Romany drink Ma. always had by her, helped Jenny, but in any case she had a reasonable birth, although perhaps Jenny might not agree, but very soon a proud Jenny, cleaned up, but tired was able to show Rob his seven pound son. Of course the telephone was soon used to tell Rob's parents the wonderful news and in three hours two proud and happy Grandparents sat by the bed. After a good nights sleep Jenny announced that the baby boy, hopefully heir to the Graham farm, should be Christened David Robin Graham.

Merri, Gil, Tom, Frank and so many others came to visit, until the doctor, always called by Ma. usually after the birth, as a safety measure, decided no more visitors for two days. Jenny and Rob had their new son to themselves, blissfully happy they spent the two days planning David's future, both knew if Andrew married and produced a son perhaps he would take the inheritance but Rob considered this very unlikely. With Robs parents returned to the farm, Andrew came loaded with gifts for his nephew, he was so happy, telling Jenny how proud he would be to eventually help David become a good farmer and how happy it made him not to feel under pressure to marry just to produce a heir. Rob was now well in charge of Staunton Garage, still not having enough cars or tractors from Ford in Manchester to sell, but even so profits from fuel, oil and service were holding up well. Bertie, who had been invalided out of the army before the war ended, due to the loss of his hand, was now the foreman with two mechanics and a boy for the workshop, the lady who had charge of the parts counter since before the war was still doing that job. The young lady who had looked after the accounts had left to become one of the post war expectant mums and so Jenny had taken over the finance chair. Bertie's wife Pip had for several years been responsible for cleaning new vehicles and customers vehicles coming in for service. Bertie and Pip had been married for two years and had no sign yet, of a family arriving, both considered this strange because during their time of courting, before marriage, they had often been careless about just when they made love, often Pip saying" well that must mean I am having a baby", but it never happened. Now after two happy careless years of marriage, it seemed a baby would never come, Pip and Jenny were good friends from the days when Pip lived in Johnsons farm, so Pip was an early and jealous, in a happy way, visitor to see Jenny and David, just let me hold him Pip said, he is so lovely. Holding him and looking at him, Pip told Jenny how lucky she was, "Oh I know that, but when are you going to have a baby", Jenny enquired, Pip looking into David's eyes suggested perhaps soon, if David can produce a mothering instinct like the one I feel now.

In mid September Gil arrived driven by Tom, "I feel it is time I moved in mum", she told Jane, Merri was also uneasy but hoping it would soon be over. A few days later Gil, with some difficulty and the attendance of the doctor to help with a few stitches, was able to hold her son, James Frank Simpson. Ellenor could not wait to take them home, she was like a dog with two tails. Twenty four hours later Merri produced, without difficulty or delay a daughter, Julie Jane

Johnson, soon to be known to all as Jay, both new mums were soon sitting together quite often feeding their babies and comparing notes about their birth and the habits quickly being acquired by both babies.

Eventually Gil returned to the Simpson home, Merri with Jay and Tom occupied his room, the night feeds, Tom found, were a good time to kiss and cuddle, so many a midnight hour passed with love and tender actions. By the end of October these, almost courting sessions had been taken over by much more serious love making, Merri claiming she would not be caught for another baby whilst she was feeding Jay. Both Girls were still breast feeding but as time went on the feeds were gradually being supplemented by a bottle. Jane Knowles had agreed to take over the nursery, watched over by Jane and Merri, and had agreed to live in the farmhouse. Ellenor was happy to be nursemaid for Gil and between them they could easily handle the bookkeeping for the Simpson business.

The corn harvest was finished, Merri was now doing some lorry driving during the day and most of the farm staff were gathering the root harvest. No less than one hundred acres of swedes, mangolds and potatoes were to be harvested, cold mornings, short days and rain, not to mention mud, made the 1919 root harvest a very difficult and unpleasant time. During that period both Tom and Joe spent many days carting the root crops to the farm, whilst Billy and Harry were ploughing with the Fordson tractors, Each Sunday morning Joe and Tom would service the tractors, cleaning trembler coil points, plugs and fuel lines, also changing the engine oil, each driver was responsible for greasing each morning and checking oil levels. With this kind of effort put into caring for them the Fordsons were proving both reliable and efficient. Every other night Tom or Joe would clean the distributor roller at the front of the engine, this important item was subject to rapid wear if neglected and was the most unreliable part of the tractor if allowed to run in dirt or dust.

With two hundred acres ploughed, Tom suggested he should use one of the old Mogul tractors to prepare the ground for seeding the winter wheat, this they agreed was a good idea, so that the Fordsons could keep up with the winter ploughing programme. The short days meant starting at daybreak and working until it was too dark to see, the root harvesters were doing this anyway. Merri usually took Tom his midday meal and drove the tractor whilst he ate, in the afternoon she would take him a drink and stay to ride on the tractor as it went up and down the field, later walking home with him in the darkness. Jane was now doing almost all the kitchen work, Ma. helping but also spending time in the nursery with Jay and Jane Knowles, this led to Ma. reading or sewing in the nursery and Jane Knowles working part of the day in the kitchen helping Jane.

One day a telephone call from the estate office came requesting Joe to go and speak with the new estate manager, this was quite unexpected, Josh Symonds the estate manager for many years had retired and a new man had taken over. When Joe and Tom arrived at the office Lord Jensen himself was there to greet them and introduce his new manager, James Thurlow, a young man about twenty nine years old. He was a friend from Lord jensen's army days and had studied land and forestry management before the war. His approach was friendly as his Lordship introduced Joe and Tom, telling James that the Johnsons were one of the estates star tenants, not only were they never late with the rent but also helped with making the pheasant shoot a success. Of course, Lord Jensen told James, I might be here on crutches if Joe's daughter had not been both ruthless and such a good nurse when I was wounded in France. Lord Jensen left the office and James Thurlow turned to the Johnson's, he told them the rent dinner was being restarted this coming November and an invitation would be with them shortly. Now to business, James said, telling them that the old army camp was being returned to the estate by the War Office. This to include a number of buildings on the side of the road farmed by Jensen Estates. On the other side, that on which Johnsons farm was situated, were three large wooden buildings and James suggested if the fifteen acre field in which they stood were to be rented to Johnsons farm the three buildings would be included. Joe soon recognised this would give Johnsons farm access to both sides of the river and also join up with land belonging to Riverside farm, already rented from the estate. This seemed to Joe a good deal but wishing to consult with Tom, Jane and Ma. privately, he told James he would say yes, but in case the owners of Johnsons farm disagreed he would confirm and indeed sign an agreement the next day, if James so wished.

Whilst Joe and Tom were visiting the estate office, Merri took the morning meat supply and eggs to the dairy in Little Staunton, Merri visited the dairy most mornings, of course that had been her home until she had married Tom. Tessa, her mother made Merri welcome, demanding all the news of her Granddaughter Jay. With the Ford unloaded Merri left to call on Gil who had arranged to travel back to the farm in the lorry, so that Jane could see her Grandson James. Walking into the Simpson kitchen Gil told Merri that mother had telephoned to see if they would call on Jenny to make sure she was OK, Rob was ill with his chest again and Jane wanted the two girls to call on Jenny in case she needed any help. Drawing up on the garage front, Merri asked Pip if Jenny was there or at home, Pip informed her jenny was in the office with David. Walking back to the lorry, Merri asked Gil if she was coming to see Jenny, "Oh yes I am, but look at the new petrol pump, no more pouring petrol from tins now eh". With David asleep, Jenny was working on the garage finances, already two days behind with bookkeeping, Jenny told them. There was very little they could do at the moment and Jenny hoped Rob would soon be able to breath a little easier, if he were to be in bed for too long, then Jenny told them she may be glad of some assistance.

Back at the farm Gil took James into the kitchen where he was duly fawned over and held by a loving Grandmother and Great Grandmother, soon he was taken to the nursery where he joined Jay in the care of Jane knowles. Joe explained the visit to the estate office over the midday meal, Jane said she could understand the estate making the offer, it would be less costly to the estate to have Johnsons farm clear up the army camp, with its roads and sheds. Joe looked at his wife with a smile, "cannot you think of a good use for it in its present form" he asked, " anyway I must go and get the seed drill ready, we could start drilling the wheat tomorrow, I will tell you about the army camp to-night". With Tom away to the Mogul tractor preparing a twenty acre field for the wheat, the four ladies soon washed up, Ma. and Young Jane retired to the nursery with bottles for the babies, whilst Jane asked Gil and Merri to come into the office. Sitting together, Jane asked if either of them had given thought to how soon they might have the next baby, " goodness mum, I am still feeding James", Gil told her," yes I know and Merri is still feeding Jay, but neither of you are doing so completely and I feel sure you are both likely to fall for another baby quite soon now, especially as you feel the need for your men growing, you may say I shall not be tempted again, but you will be you know and probably just at the most dangerous

29

time of the month", Merri looked at Jane, "how can we calculate when it is dangerous to make love until our monthly time starts again. Tom and I are already enjoying a lovely free time, but I am expecting each week to have warning to be careful in the future", " and so am I Gil told Jane", " well if you are already enjoying your love life so much be prepared to have another baby very soon, after all you may become pregnant before you have a monthly period", " do you think that is possible", Gil asked, Jane left them in no doubt that she thought it was certainly so. Merri told Jane that came as something of a shock, she had expected to have some warning before it became dangerous to make love.

Both girls decided they must be very careful now after Jane's warning, "what more careful than on your Honeymoon ", Jane asked, with a smile, "are you aware that there are protectors available that are reasonably reliable I can tell you where to obtain some, if you wish". " Tell me more ", Merri said "well I shall have to be very crude", Jane told them, going on to say, they are like sausage skins, tied at one end and worn by the man, but are apparently very reliable. Gil burst out laughing, then sang roll up, roll up a sausage or a baby, at that they all burst out laughing again. Becoming serious again Jane explained " they are made from the same part of the pig that sausage skins are made from and who has more pigs than most, yes of course, Riverside farm". Gil asked why they were not told about them before they were married, Jane said she was sorry about that but felt it better for the girls health and the basis for a stable marriage that at first nature should be allowed to make what arrangements it thought best, and how lovely those arrangements had worked out. "So you and dad used them" said Gil, Jane told her that they had used nothing for ten years now, they had not worried whether a baby came or not, in fact nothing had happened and if it did Jane was not concerned. Now Jane said she was resigned to loving her grandchildren, "So what do we do now", asked Merri, Jane suggested they go and see Meg at Riverside and let her explain about the protectors she made. "Hey wait a minute, if they are so reliable how come Meg herself has a baby", asked Gil, but no one has ever suggested they are totally reliable Gil was told, "But I will let you into a little secret, they worked for ten years for Meg until our harvest supper two years ago, Meg had rather too much wine and she thinks they forgot to use a protector, and that is exactly what happened to me when Tom came along", Jane told them. "Surely you were not drunk", Merri enquired, " I am so ashamed to admit it but on two occasions I needed Joe to help me walk, perhaps not drunk but certainly happy", Jane told them. Gil is the result of the first occasion and Tom the second. "Ah Gil said, so if we go out one night and get you sloshed we may still get another little brother", "yes well, I suppose so laughed Jane, but probably you will be in the same state so it might be a case of then there were three". Are you going to ring Meg Merri enquired, I think we should take all the care we can. As Gil and Merri left Meg, with all the information she could give them, they sat for a few minutes talking in the lorry cab, are you going to use one", Merri asked, Gil told her that Ellenor had told her to take care when she had weaned James, the chemical reaction of producing milk stops the production of eggs to make babes, so Gil was going to use them after her first monthly period gave her guidance as to when it might be essential to use a protector. Merri agreed but pointed out that cows could still be put in calf even though they were producing a lot of milk, still I suppose they must be different to us.

That night in the office Joe explained his thoughts about the army camp, they listened to him say that the site lay on the junction with the trunk road to London, already a busy road and the lane leading into Jensen and Little Staunton. Joe thought the estate believed Johnsons farm would use the sheds for storage, but he thought it was an ideal site for a petrol pump, with oil and a few spare parts, surely one shed could be developed into a tea shop with home made cakes and meats to make sandwiches from Riverside. In the morning he was going to speak to the councilor in Little Staunton and then to James in the estate office. " Another of your mad schemes", Jane said, leaving him in no doubt that the others had worked so she expected this to do so. Jane did not think she wanted to work in a tea shop, neither did Joe, but he thought it was a venture that ought to be run by Staunton Garage. One problem was that Rob's health seemed very bad, Joe had no doubt Jenny would be keen on the idea but would Rob feel able to respond to the challenge.

With hindsight Joe believed they had sold Rob the twenty one per cent of the garage with too much haste, but maybe he could talk to Gil and either buy part of her shares or obtain a positive agreement that Gil would always back the farm share in the garage. Tom , looking at his Dad, asked where these ideas came from, admitting he felt quite ashamed that he had not thought of using the site as a petrol station. Jane soon told him not to worry, his father always had silly ideas, but most of them seemed to make money, Jane had no doubt that Tom would be just as unusual as his Dad in due course. Tom suggested his silly idea might well be that they buy a threshing set, the one Frank and Gil had sold, it was not doing very well. The new owners were not able to produce the quality of grain, nor were they willing to work every day, some customers had already changed to a new contractor. Tom had heard they were asking three hundred pounds for it, without the tractor.

Who told you, Joe enquired, Tom had been to visit a friend and had met the owners brother there, Joe looked at Ma. and jane, shall we send Tom to offer a little less, we need our threshing done well. They agreed, Tom thought that Rory Deane and the estate farm would sign up with them, giving two months threshing, mostly in the winter months, thus Johnsons farm would get its own threshing done almost for nothing. " Marvellous", Jane cried " there is two of them at it now, which will suggest buying the houses of parliament to use as a grain store I wonder",

That night as Jay lay in Merri's arms gently taking her night feed, Merri told Tom about her visit to Meg, when Jay had gently gurgled herself to sleep, Merri showed Tom one of the protectors. It was very thin and slightly veined, neatly knotted at one end and rolled from the other until it was quite short. Talking and looking at this unusual thing, Tom could feel himself becoming very much aroused, Merri smiling, suggested it it was not a delicate protector he needed but a piece of motor tyre to keep him in check. By this time they were both aroused, especially so after the very close and loving kisses they were sharing. Eventually Tom, with the protector in place, lay by a very willing affectionate and urgent Merri, Tom had no nightshirt on and with the nightgown of Merri gently removed, they were soon as close together as two lovers can be. It was only a short time before they both knew, almost as one, that the protector was spoiling the pleasure they had grown to enjoy. As Tom gently withdrew, Merri removed it and Tom resumed his lovemaking, soon they were both satisfied and sleepy. The next morning they spoke about how difficult it would be to use the protectors, but both agreed it was at least better than Merri becoming pregnant too often, as would surely happen if they were not very careful.

Later that morning Merri drove Joe into Little Staunton and whilst she unloaded at the dairy, joe walked to the council offices. There he was able to talk to the officer responsible for building, a man he knew quite well, explaining what he wanted to do with the old army camp, the officer told him there were no bylaws to say he could not use the buildings as he suggested. But he must remember there must be proper access from the trunk road and he must meet all the proper health regulations that restaurants were subject to. Rejoining Merri at the dairy they set off on the return journey, whilst joe had been visiting the council office, Merri had paid a quick visit to Gil, their experience had been the same as Merri's, that the protector was a disaster to the love life that they were experiencing. Frank decided it was better to avoid all loving contact when Gil told him that was necessary, rather than use such passion killers. The only thing is that I need him so much sometimes it may be that I tempt him to go beyond what is safe, Gil told her. Merri agreed knowing full well there was no way she would have stopped Tom from the contact she so desired the previous night, I only hope we can soon calculate our monthly times, Merri told Gil, saying she was becoming worried how demanding her feelings were becoming.

During the afternoon Joe visited the estate, James showed him in to his office and Joe told him they all agreed that the extra fifteen acres should be added to Johnsons farm, a simple agreement was then signed by Joe on behalf of the farm. Joe then explained that although the army sheds would be useful to Johnsons farm for storage, Joe had other ideas in his head. He then explained how they would like to use about three acres for selling petrol and perhaps using one of the buildings for a tea room and shop selling produce from the farm. Indeed any produce from the village, Jam, fruit or cakes and pies which perhaps one of the village ladies may be happy to supply and so help out her income. You know of course our family jointly owns the Ford garage in Little Staunton and it seemed to me, that company should run the corner site, if you agree it may be used for that purpose. James looked at Joe, saying how Lord Jensen had told him that Joe was full of unusual ideas and that most of them worked. Certainly I will tell his Lordship what you want to do, but I am sure he will not object so long as you meet any obligations the council put on you. Of course it will no longer be classed as agricultural land, so you must expect to pay a commercial rate of some kind.

"Now to another subject", James said, "you know of course that on the plot of land on the other corner of Jensen lane there are four more army huts and further into the field is a small sewage disposal plant". It appears that there has been an agreement made that the council will take over the plant and will pay part of the cost of a sewer through Jensen, if Lord Jensen and his tenants will also meet some of the cost, thus Jensen village will be a better place to live. Joe was surprised at this development, feeling certain the old Lord Jensen would never have been willing to spend that kind of money, James explained that with the rent dinner invitation would be an announcement of this new main drain and a cost to each tennant. You will also realise, James told him that across the main road is the larger part of the old army camp, including about twenty five sheds and service roads. Lord Jensen has the war office agreement that if he will take down the sheds then the war office will remove all the trace of the roads and pay the estate to restore the site to pasture land.

Two nights later Joe having made sure Rob was now fit

enough to attend, had the agreement of the garage shareholders that they should meet in the farm office, to discuss the corner site development. With them all assembled, including Tom and Merri, Joe set out the proposal for the corner site to be used as a petrol and spare parts stop and for one of the sheds to be used as a tea room. Gil asked if this was confidential, Joe told her it was not, going on to say that although Gil had married into what, perhaps, on some occasions might be a rival in trade, he would on some things ask Gil to keep information to herself, but not today. After lengthy discussion they agreed that the opportunity was good, there being no similar development within six miles in either direction, Joe had purposely driven the trunk road to check this. Joe also suggested the corner site, in future years, could be developed into a lorry depot. leaving the garage in Little Staunton to be a car only site. He explained there were already many lorries travelling the road, also it was not unusual to see one broken down or with a flat tyre, some of course were still using solid tyres, but the days of those were surely numbered.

Jenny was asked how the garage finances were, was any money available for expansion and, indeed who thought expansion desirable. Jenny explained that Rob and herself were both taking a low weekly wage because they were full time employees, Gil and Johnsons farm might expect to receive a small dividend at the end of the year, but in all, the bank account stood at only 1.500 pounds, which was the minimum they considered safe, especially in view of the fact that Ford might soon start allocating cars , lorries or tractors to them. After more discussion Joe suggested taking a loan from the bank, asking Rob if he felt able to agree and if so they would visit the bank together, Joe suggested two thousand pounds might fill the need.

They agreed on that course of action and Rob suggested he would see if the petrol company would contribute to the supply of petrol facilities, in exchange for a deal to sell only their petrol and oil. Turning to Tom Joe asked if he had made any progress with the threshing machine, "Oh yes I have bought it", tom told them, looking at Tom in surprise Merri asked when had he seen the owner, " this afternoon when I fetched the harrow spares", Tom told her. Turning to Ma. he asked if she had 250 pounds in cash, because he had bought it for 270 in cash if he would deliver it to the farm in the morning. I had to borrow twenty pounds from the dairy to pay a deposit and make sure he did not change his mind. Jane looked at her son, realising how much he was like his Dad, Ma joined in to say she was pleased Tom was taking responsibility, anyway Joe had never done very much wrong and if Tom took after him they would all be proud of him. The question now is she told them, how much should they advance to Tom, so any time he goes to market or to a sale he has money in his pocket to buy anything available that would be good for the farm, Ma. thought Tom should always have twenty pounds in his pocket to secure a bargain if he saw one, that also was agreed.

After all the visitors had left and the evening cup of cocoa taken, Jane and Merri cleared the kitchen and prepared it for the morning, Ma. had already retired. Jane and Joe stayed to lock the outside door as Merri and Tom climbed the stairs, hand in hand, Merri smiling told Tom how proud she was to see him becoming more and more involved with the farm management. Jane followed and finally Joe, candle stick in hand he extinguished the paraffin lamp in the kitchen, also the one in the hall and with the old house settling to peace and darkness Joe joined his wife in their bedroom. Tom and Merri closed the bedroom door behind them, walking over to the cot with their candle, Tom held it high so they had a good view of Jay, sound asleep," isn't she beautiful", Merri said, Tom's reply was instant, "just like her mum". Merri turned to him, putting her arms around his neck, " I love you so much Tom", she kissed him passionately, after a few moments they broke away, took off their clothes and soon were lying together, renewing the kiss of a few minutes before. It took only a short time before Merri, now so used to the freedom she enjoyed to make love, moved closer to Tom and with almost a years practice behind her, she was very plainly signalling " come and give us both the pleasure we have enjoyed so much". Tom responded strongly at first, then suddenly abandoned his activities and lay beside her, questioning what they were doing.

Tom was gently seeking assurance from Merri that it really was safe to make love so freely and so often, pointing out that it was a long time since Jay was born and surely they must be careful not to have Merri caught with another baby so soon after Jay. Tom explained he was enjoying the same wonderful feeling he had enjoyed on their honeymoon, the feelings they had so carelessly enjoyed and which had given them Jay. Merri, so very reluctant to abandon their pleasure, eventually agreed that perhaps they should wait for a while to see if her period would start and then they could calculate when it was safe to make love. Eventually lying so close they drifted off to sleep, about two o'clock Jay whimpered, she rarely cried, so Tom lit the candle and brought a half awake baby girl to her mother for the night feed. As they lay together in bed, Jay lazily sucking Merri's breast, there was an exclamation from Merri, telling Tom what a mucky kid he had produced, not only did her nappy want changing but half the milk she was sucking was being spilt all over mum.

Tom love, do me a favour and fetch a jug of warm water from the kitchen, or I shall smell for the rest of the night. With nappy changed and Jay dozing back in her cot, Tom returned with the water. Pouring some into the wash stand basin, he carefully cooled it by adding cold from the jug that was always full, standing by the basin. Merri now naked in the cold bedroom, clean nightie ready on the bed, walked to the wash stand where Tom already had a soapy flannel ready. "Come here, hold this towel whilst I clean you up", he told her, warm flannel, smooth soap and Tom's gentle touch, soon had Merri, not only clean but more demanding than ever. Her smooth warm body had the most desperately passionate effect on Tom and as Merri slipped into a still warm bed Tom pulled his night shirt over his head and joined his wife in another world, eventually, totally spent, lovely and warm they lay together, occasionally their lips met, but soon they fell asleep. As the alarm clock called them, Merri looked at Tom, " goodness what a short night", she told him. Will it be along summer for you, Tom asked, reminding her she had told them she would drive the tractor for the next years corn cutting, leaving her in no doubt that many nights like the last one and there would be no corn cutting for her. "Surely I cannot be having another baby so soon", Merri asked, Tom suggested she surely would and very soon, if they carried on in such a loving way.

After breakfast, Tom and Joe set the newly arrived threshing set in the horse yard and paid the driver the required cash, he drove away on the Titan tractor, steam engine type wheels scrunching over the horse yard gravel and the threshing set, drum, straw chopper and straw bundler were left for the Johnsons inspection. It was obvious from the start that the outfit had been badly neglected, either through idleness or ignorance, it made little difference, there was a lot of work to do on the set, but of course they had bought it quite cheaply. "The best thing we can do is ask Frank to come and inspect it", Joe said. Frank came in the afternoon with Gil and James, both Frank and Gil were appalled at the condition of the set, especially after only having sold it two years ago.

The bearings seemed to have been well greased, so well that the ribbons of oil running down from each bearing was covered in chaff and dust like flies on a fly paper. Belts were polished and slippery, showing no sign of being treated with Stockholm tar and resin to give them good grip. The fold out boards on top of the drum were damaged and several of the metal clasps broken, being replaced with binder twine. Inside the machine was dirty and one of the riddles that oscillated, to grade the corn out from the short pieces of straw and chaff, had a hole in it, thus all sorts of rubbish was allowed through, this was probably why the set now had a reputation for producing a bad sample of grain. Luckily the beater bars and the concave, very expensive parts, seemed alright, much to Gil's annoyance the feeder pit, in which she had stood for so long during the war years, was almost full of wet straw and rotten grain. The safety bar that Joe had made, so it was difficult to fall into the revolving machinery, had disappeared and with paint peeling, it was easy to see the machine had a bad home. The straw bundler had dirty and rusted twine runs, blunt knotter knife and damaged twine jaws, so it must have miss tied as many bundles as it tied. The straw chopper had a blunt and damaged chopper blade and must have taken a lot more power to drive it than it should have. Even so Joe and Tom were pleased with the purchase, Frank made a list of the spares needed and agreed to keep visiting to offer some assistance and advice.

The original Mogul tractor that had been used to drive the threshing outfit before the Titan had been purchased, was to be used to drive it again, so Frank did an examination of that but found very little wrong with it. In the meantime Gil had returned to the kitchen and Joined Merri with Jane, as the three sat with a cup of tea Merri described how Jay was rejecting her night feed, Gil could understand what Merri was saying, but had not experienced it Quite so badly. Jane soon told them the night feed should be dropped and suggested a night bottle, to replace the breast feed, with milk and water, eventually working the mixture to almost pure water after a week or so. Then, hopefully the children would not bother waking for such an unpalatable mixture. Now, Jane told them we get to the difficult bit, I can give you a herbal drink that Aunt Annarita taught me to produce, it quickly dried up my milk supply and will, no doubt do the same for you, but if you believe in the old wives tale about not being caught for a baby whilst breast feeding, I do not by the way, you must be very careful when you are in bed with your Husband's. Of course you may by now be used to not going too far, but once you have stopped feeding your baby yourself, nature soon realises that now is the time to produce another little human being, so be warned, use your protectors and keep a good supply handy.

Later, before Gil left for home, Merri asked how her love life was, brilliant Gil told her, yes so is mine Merri said, but Tom was beginning to think they must soon stop and give more thought to being much more careful, Gil thought they might soon have the monthly time coming, once the breast feeding had stopped and so then it might be easier to calculate when it would be unwise to make love freely. Merri laughing, suggested knowing when it would be unwise to make love and actually doing something about it were two different things.

The invitation to the rent dinner and the announcement of the new sewage system duly arrived, the cost to Johnsons farm to be connected was stated as two hundred and fifty pounds. Joe was certain they must not only pay for the sewer connection, but should spend some money on the farm house to obtain the maximum gain from this modern development. This was the first rent dinner provided by Lord Jensen since before the war, Ma. of course received an invitation, as did Jane and Joe, this year the event was held in the ballroom in Jensen Manor. Just as in pre-war years each tennant was greeted by the butler holding a silver salver into which the tennant placed his named envelope containing the rent for the property, with his agreement, or otherwise to the sewer scheme, a glass of sherry was then presented and the guests were free to talk and admire the beautiful entrance hall. Soon the butler announced that dinner was served, the guests stood by their named places until Lord Jensen entered to his ornate chair at the head of the table. The vicar, Rev. Williams, brought the Lords blessing to the table and the meal was then served. Jane was surprised to see the vicars new wife eating in a very coarse way and drink a considerable quantity of wine, later when the ladies had withdrawn into an adjacent lounge, again was surprised to see her take three glasses of port.

Later that evening Joe reminded Jane of the first rent dinner they had attended and how difficult she had found it to walk home, memories, Jane told Joe, reminding him how the wine waiter had kept topping up the glasses of the young women. This must have been his way of gaining pleasure from watching young women gradually, and almost without knowing, become increasingly under the influence. "I must say that I never knew what a state I was in until we set off home, but of course that was almost twenty years ago" Jane told him " and if I remember correctly we really did enjoy our night together when we did reach home". " I wonder if the Rev. Williams wife will enjoy her night as much as I enjoyed mine all those years ago, she must have been as bad as I was, judging by the amount of wine and port she drank tonight", Joe agreed, he had noticed her taking quite a lot of wine at the table.

The next evening Joe surprised everyone by enlarging on his statement that they must, in his opinion, spend some money on Johnsons farm house. His idea was to coincide with the laying of the new sewer, the kitchen stove was to be updated so it could provide hot water, that water should be available on all sinks and wash basins. The nursery should have a wash basin fitted with hot and cold water, a bath not being considered necessary because the current bathroom was in the next room. The three main bedrooms should each have a wash basin, bath and toilet fitted, Joe believed they were big enough to fit a partition to accommodate this, in addition, the current bathroom must have a toilet fitted and the outside staff toilet must also be connected to the new sewer.

The estimate for this work, in Joe's opinion was about six hundred pounds and he asked for their agreement to call in a plumber to give a quotation for the work. Joe's only regret was that they did not yet have a supply of electricity in the village or he would have suggested that the house be fully wired at this time. Ma. and Jane, looking at Joe together, reminded him that a relatively short time ago, he was the one who had suggested they conserve capital, because the post war years were unlikely to yield the profit that the war years had. "Yeas I know but it will never be so easy again to modernise our home, certainly I would not suggest that we break into our reserves, but we have just completed the heaviest corn harvest we have ever had. The price of wheat is tending to drop, it will, in my opinion be worth much less money in spring. We have the threshing machine and just one of those big wheat stacks will pay for the farmhouse modernisation. We also have the christmas trade coming and this year, again, it shows real signs of growth. I was talking to Bill at the dairy and he thinks the orders for poultry and meat is already ten per cent over last year.

Joe left them in no doubt that he thought the wheat should be threshed and as much as possible sold whilst the price was still almost at its wartime high. Joe felt that with no submarines to threaten the merchant ships crossing from America there would soon be boat loads of good hard wheat arriving in English ports. Tom asked if they had read the newspapers lately, the government, showing a grateful nation that it intended, never again, to allow farmers and farm workers to sink into financial disaster was suggesting a basic price for farm produce, below which prices could not fall. The government intended to intervene if prices fell too much, until they had again stabilised. Tom thought this would mean a minimum price being set and he was in no doubt that the minimum price would quickly become a normal price, of course the suggested minimum was not yet set, but current opinion in the farming press led Tom to believe, if that ever happened, to days price for wheat might decrease by forty per cent.

Tom's ideas took them all by surprise, no one had realised that he was taking the farm so seriously, but his ideas matched those of his Dad. It was agreed that as soon as the wheat crop for next year was set, they would thresh as much as possible of this years wheat, along with oats, barley and beans for stock feed, before the set left home to thresh anyone else's stacks. The estate farm and Rory Deane had both decided the Johnson farm threshing set should thresh their corn stacks. The next problem was how to staff the thresher, it would need a feeder to put the sheaves through the drum, a driver to move it who would also feed the chopper, if anyone wanted their straw chopping into small pieces for animal feed. He would also keep watch on all the many parts that might malfunction. One other person was desirable who would stand on the drum and take each sheaf of corn from the person on the stack, cut the string around the sheaf and pass it to the feeder. Who must feed the machine a continuous stream of corn as fast as possible, without slowing the machine by giving it too much.

The characteristic hum from the machine told all the workers when the feeder had everything right, too light the hum and the customer was not getting the maximum output, an uneven hum, with perhaps, some "bumps" from the machine would mean uneven and overfeeding, leading to a bad sample of threshed grain in the sacks. A deep steady hum meant a good feeder and a slick sheaf string cutter, supplying the drum feeder with an ample and smooth supply of stringless sheaves. This was why the two people on the drum should both understand the job and be very skilled at it. Who will fill these positions was the question, Tom would certainly wish to drive the outfit, but Joe soon told him, he should not be tied up every day, as a future farmer his job should be easily changed day by day. So that any problem that came along could be dealt with, of course it was important that Tom knew how to use the machine but it was wrong to tie him to it.

Joe suggested that Billy Arnold be the threshing machine operator, Tom could drive Billy's tractor if the winter ploughing was not finished, by doing this, Tom could leave the ploughing for a day if necessary. "How about asking Jill Worsley if she would work the weeks when the machine was in action, as drum feeder, Jane Knowles in the nursery could look after her children if Jill agreed Jane suggested.

The other person to work with the feeder could, perhaps be Elizabeth Knowles from Moorside farm, Joe thought he should ask them the following day, with the idea that everyone could start steadily in two days time to set the machine, under the guidance of Frank, ready to start serious work the next day. The next morning Joe walked round to see Jill, who told him she would just love to work on the threshing set, but felt she must make the decision with Bill, her husband. She told Joe she felt happy to leave the children with Jane Knowles in the farmhouse, she also told him it would be wonderful to earn some money.

Talking with Jim and Jessie Knowles, Joe soon had their agreement to his idea, so long as Elizabeth agreed. They explained that Elizabeth had taken to setting snares with Walter Lieber, the German Ex prisoner, who lived in the Bothy at Johnsons farm. They felt perhaps there might be a suggestion of romance in the air, this was a surprise to Joe who had pride in knowing everything that went on, but that situation had escaped him. "How would you feel about having a German for a son in law", Joe asked "Oh we like him but wish we knew him a little better", Jessie told Joe. Before he left them Joe suggested that if Elizabeth agreed she should visit Jane to have one of the farm overalls fitted, because they all felt long skirts or dresses were not appropriate wear with moving machinery.

Just before Joe left Moorside Jessie asked if he would be offended by Jessie offering Walter a room in Moorside, she explained that if Elizabeth was indeed, taken with him it might be a good idea if they could all get to know him well. Jessie also suggested that it must be terribly cold in the Bothy during the mid-winter months so it was also a humanitarian gesture. Joe reminded her that he and Jane had been snaring rabbits both before and after they were married, the experiences had been wonderful, but better done after marriage. There was, of course the case of Janette and Rory Deane who had to marry in rather a hurry. Was Jessie really sure about what she was proposing, Jessie assured Joe that she and her daughter were very close and open with one another, Jessie felt happier watching whatever might develop by having them both living in the house. During the afternoon Elizabeth came to see Jane and was fitted out with the traditional bib and brace overalls, 3 pairs, 3 white high neck vests and several pairs of the matching knickers. Elizabeth told Jane she had never worn underwear like that before, but Jane assured her she would realise how good it was as soon as they started to thresh barley.

CHAPTER TWO

Joe left Moorside farm to visit Jenny and Rob, he was soon invited to join them for a sandwich lunch, Joe and Rob had an appointment with the new bank manager, who was due to replace Mr. Appleyard in two weeks time. The appointment was for 2.30 pm. and Joe was hoping that Mr. Clement Hanson would soon become as helpful as Mr. Appleyard had been over the years. Joe and Rob arriving a few minutes early, were shown into the managers office where both old and new managers had a desk. Introductions were made and Mr. appleyard explained that Mr. Hanson was now making all the decisions, but he, Mr Appleyard, was acting in an advisory capacity. Mr. Hanson, a sharp featured man, immaculately dressed, with a rather light covering of hair on his head, well slicked back had a rather slow but high pitched voice and appeared to Joe a typical hard financier.

Mr. Hanson explained that he had studied the files on Johnsons farm and had nothing but admiration for the way the account had flourished and how the farm had always met its targets, even in the indifferent financial climate experienced before the war. He could also see Mr. Appleyard had played his part in the growth of the farm and he hoped to continue in a like manner. Apart from the need to meet his important customers, Mr. Hanson understood from the telephone that Joe, representing the largest share holder and Mr. Graham, the chief executive of Staunton Garage, had a proposal to make about future expansion and the need to finance it.

Rob, well briefed by Joe, explained about the site on the

trunk road and their plans to develop it, Rob also told Mr. Hanson how traffic was growing rapidly and that many breakdowns and punctures were appearing within the ten mile stretch that the new development might cover. Rob also explained that the petrol company would install fuel dispensing pumps and lubricating facilities, whilst Ford Motor Company had agreed to erect a large sign on the site. However to start the new site off in a business like way they both estimated about two thousand pounds would be needed, this could be paid back in five years time, assuming current interest rates were maintained. After some discussion, during which Mr. Hanson showed he was a capable and careful bank manager, turned to them and said he could grant the request for two thousand pounds on condition that Johnsons farm would act as guarantor for the loan to Staunton Garage.

There the matter was left for Joe to obtain the consent of the shareholders in Johnsons farm, whilst Rob was to do likewise with the garage shareholders. Mr. Appleyard suggested the loan should be available immediately and an agreement signed by all parties in a few days time. Mr. Hanson agreed and a further meeting to sign the paperwork was arranged for three days time. With the agreement signed and some money already allocated to making a good entrance to the site, the highway authority were consulted. They would approve the entrance and exit, but only they could do the work, of course at Staunton Garage expense. Their work would cease at the boundary between the highway and private land, after that the private individual could make what road surface they wished.

In the meantime the threshing set had been placed by one of the wheat stacks, under the instructions of Frank, he took time to explain how important it was to use a spirit level to ensure the machine was set exactly level, there were jacks and blocks for this purpose. Tom and Billy assumed that with so many moving parts the thresher would suffer premature wear if sited unevenly. Frank confirmed that, but told them the importance of being level was mainly so an even spread of grain, chaff and broken straw was dispersed right across the riddles, allowing the draught from the fan to blow away the chaff and straw bits, whilst the heavier grain passed through the riddle. There are so many adjustments on a threshing machine that whole books have been written about them, but at the base, nothing works well if the machine is not level.

Gil had arrived with Frank, wearing her overalls, Gil had not worn them for twelve months and was enjoying the sensation of working clothes again. Gil, Elizabeth and Jill were soon on the top of the machine and as sheaves were fed from the stack, Gil explained how the string bands should be cut. Using a sharp knife, fastened with a loop of string around the wrist so there was no chance it could accidentally fall into the machine. The cut string was held in the hand until quite a bundle had accumulated and then dropped to the floor to be picked up later, the sheaf, now loose was passed to the feeder who smoothly and fast, fed it into the drum. Whilst the three girls were on the machine being fed slowly with sheaves from the stack, Gil was trying to help Jill and Elizabeth streamline their actions so in the near future they could feed the drum to its maximum capacity. Whilst this was going on Frank was showing Tom and Billy some of the many adjustments necessary to always ensure a good sample of grain was obtained. Of course heavy grain, such as beans, needed one setting, medium grain such as wheat needed another and light grain such as oats needed yet another setting. Eventually when Frank was satisfied with the quality of grain produced, he climbed the ladder to the feeder platform, there he asked for a quicker supply of sheaves from the stack and for twenty minutes he, cutting bands and Gil feeding the sheaves into the voracious machine, worked it to its maximum capacity. The grain sacks were filling quickly, the chaff discharged under the machine, suddenly made the chaff carriers almost run to carry it away and the straw bundles from the rear of the machine arrived on the stack much quicker, in fact even on a cold winter day everyone began to sweat.

All now left to do was for Jill and Elizabeth to find the speed Gil and Frank could produce, half an hour later the family sat in the farm kitchen talking over the mornings work, Frank and Gil decided to stay part of the afternoon just to make sure the machine continued to run well. Soon the Mogul tractor was started and as the engine speed increased, that wonderful deep hum rose from the threshing machine, the afternoons work had begun. Frank helped around the grain outlet so he could keep an eye on the quality, whilst Gil helped generally around the machine. An hour later Frank decided it was now better to leave the crew to learn on their own, so he and Gil walked to the house to collect James. Jane told them he had only just gone to sleep for his afternoon rest, so why don't you leave him here and come for your tea and then take him home tonight. This was agreed, Frank saying he could check the grain and try to answer any questions the workers might have. Frank and Gil drove home, feeling the old familiar itchy sensation from the dust that penetrated everywhere, you know Frank I still love to work on the drum, I wish it was still ours, the time I spent with you in those wartime years were so exciting and satisfying", Gil admitted that she had very soon realised she must have Frank as a husband during the first year they worked together.

Squeezing up to him, as he drove, she told him how she had longed to enjoy a love life with him, but had resisted the temptation, in case she became pregnant and made Frank feel trapped into marriage. It was not until he showed how much he cared for her that she relaxed with him, but it was very difficult to allow her feelings to run riot at first. Glancing at her, as he drove the lorry Frank remarked "now of course it does not matter what we do". Smiling at him Gil soon told him it did matter, much as she loved James, she was not going to have another baby for a while yet. Before they left the lorry cab, in the yard, Frank turned, almost as the habit had been before they were married, giving Gil a kiss, in fact a kiss much more passionate than Gil remembered in the threshing days. As she responded Frank slid his hand down her overalls and finding her thigh, gently caressed it as they kissed. Drawing apart, Gil reminded him his mother might come out any minute to collect James, "Oh no mother is working at the office all day because one of the girls has a day off". In the house they entered their own apartment, Gil telling Frank she must get rid of all the chaff and dust, " yes so must I ", Frank told her. In the kitchen Frank put his arms around Gil's waist and she responded with a kiss, this grew in passion until Gil realised she needed more, but with sharp bits of straw sticking in her, the need to be clean and comfortable seemed just as urgent. Frank unfastened her overalls and with a helping wiggle from Gil they slid to the floor, Frank's hands soon caressed her bottom and the kissing became more intense, holding him back she asked him to go and run a bath. Washing away each others dust soon had them more eager to make love than even the events in the kitchen had demanded, soon they lay on their bed, totally naked, arms around each other, with passions calling strongly for the only thing that might satisfy them. Gil drawing her head away from Franks lips looked at him, " you know Frank if we continue like this you are almost certainly, sooner or later, going to give me another baby, especially now mothers herbal drink has almost taken away my breast milk".

"Oh Gil surely we can play a little without too much risk and in any case does it really matter, surely you will not be caught for another baby so soon after James". Whilst this discussion was going on, Frank was showing his desire in the most obvious way a man can do, Gil was certainly aware of this and as he kissed her and massaged the wonderful parts of Gil he knew from experience gave her the most pleasure, he could feel her desire rising and thus her caution decreasing. Very soon with a long passionate kiss Frank slid over her, caution was no longer important, as Gil encouraged him with short sharp kisses, erect and demanding breasts, with a pair of strong arms round his waist. Frank might only have intended, as he later told her, to touch and play, but Gil soon made it so easy for him to slip into the warm loving place he had come to long for. That neither of them, at that moment, intended or wanted to stop, all caution forgotten, mother nature had taken over and was rewarding them with the kind of feelings only she could grant.

Later lying together, totally spent, a happy Frank confided

he never intended to go so far, but he had found that it was impossible to stop, "Yes I know only too well what you mean, I knew I must stop you but when the time came to do so, I just simply could not do it". Later as they dressed Gil remarked she was worried how on earth they could control their feelings in the future, she really had intended not to make real love until she had some indication when it might be safe to do so. Now all her good intentions had dissolved in one wonderful afternoon, how many more times would this happen. As far as Gil could tell it would always happen, especially when the time came that they must abstain, then probably they would find it impossible to do so.

Frank thought the problem should be ignored until another baby came along, then they must really make the protectors work, in the meantime perhaps they could just try a protector once more, Frank had been told by one of the mechanics, who had used them for two years, that they were not so bad if coated well in butter. Returning to Johnsons farm, Frank went off to see how the threshing had gone, Gil into the kitchen where Jane and Merri were sitting, walking up to the nursery to see James, Gil soon had him in her arms and was walking into Merri's bedroom, "you wanted me", Merri asked."yes, are you and Tom taking any care with your love life", Merri told Gil " I think we should do so but I must admit after one or two good resolutions had passed, we have slipped back to a, let it happen attitude". "The same with Frank and I, he thinks we should not worry but to-day, this afternoon in fact, I decided no more until I have some idea when it might be safe to make love", Gil then told Merri how she had totally ignored her resolution within two hours of making it, although perhaps nostalgia of working on the thresher again, had something to do with it. Frank says we should try the protectors again, he has been told that coating them in butter makes them feel so much better. Merri, laughing, told Gil she really was an accident waiting to happen and guessed they were both the same.

As usual, the farm Christmas trade came upon them, rabbits, cockerels, pork, eggs in large quantities, beef animals to be sold, as usual it took all the staff plus a few casual workers to prepare it all. Especially plucking and drawing the poultry, as the last minute demand increased, particularly from the dairy in London, Joe travelled miles in the lorry buying spare poultry, in all he had to purchase 400 cockerels to meet the demand. Riverside farm was also under much pressure, the demand for all products produced from the pigs was much higher than usual, Tim, Meg and family worked almost around the clock to package bacon and ham from the cold store and kill and dress pigs to provide the fresh pork and offal that seemed to be so much in demand. All this increase in trade, Joe felt was due to the many ex-service men spending their first Christmas at home in peacetime conditions, for a number of years. Also many people still had some savings from the prosperity of working over the wartime and were now set to enjoy a Christmas they had only been able to dream of whilst their families had been separated.

For two weeks before Christmas the threshing machine did not operate, so walter, now moved into Moorside farm, and Elizabeth spent many extra hours around all three farms catching rabbits, all of which could easily be sold. Boxes of pork, bacon and ham left riverside farm, baskets of eggs and rabbits and so many boxes of plucked and dressed poultry, almost a lorry load every morning left Johnsons farm to be loaded on the the train in Little Staunton destined for the London dairy. Of course Johnsons farm dairy itself, in Little Staunton, with its five milk rounds and central shop, made great demands on the same supplies. It was a very tired work force, paid off at midday on December the 24th, who took home sore hands and aching fingers, but many pound notes.

Christmas on Johnsons farm, always a time of joy and plenty, was extra special in 1919, with babies in the family again all the old joy returned. Frank and Gil came during Christmas day morning bringing presents and, of course, collecting some as well, they returned home to enjoy Ellenor's Christmas dinner. On Boxing day all the Simpson family came to Johnsons farm for the whole day, this made up, to some extent, for the absence of Rob and Jenny who had journeyed to the Graham farm, to spend a happy and wonderful Christmas with Rob's parents and brother Andrew and of course James. For four hours on Boxing day, two in the morning and two in the afternoon, Joe, Jane Tom and Merri volunteered to help Walter, the cowman and his family, milk the cows and feed the livestock also help Josie with the poultry, all jobs never ending on a farm, even at Christmas. The family also made time to attend Church on Christmas morning and again on New Years eve, returning from the church service on th latter occasion they had warm mince pies and toasted the new year of 1920 with Champagne.

After the new year, Johnsons farm annual dinner was the next social event, it was by now becoming a big event and again it was decided to hold it in the village hall. One evening Joe enquired if they were going to invite the new vicar, the Reverend Alfred Williams and his wife Judith, as

56

they always had invited the Reverend James, until he retired, to say grace before the meal. Jane supposed they really should invite them but pointed out that Judith had made something of an exhibition of herself at the rent dinner, by eating and drinking everything in site. Joe said that James Thurlow had remarked on that, but had put it down to her newly wedded status and being unaccustomed to the behaviour becoming to a vicars wife, especially one who, he understood had lived in some squalor before meeting and marrying the Rev. Williams. Joe suggested she may well improve as she becomes more accustomed to her new position, Ma. said she felt the vicar and his wife must be invited, it was a matter of good country manners to do so and that was how it was left.

Very early in the New Year Rob and Jenny came to an evening meeting in the farm study, Rob was able to tell them he had visited the three sheds on the new land now rented by Johnsons farm. His enthusiasm for the project was obvious, the council were already starting to make two entrances, one at each side of the proposed placing of the petrol pumps, which were destined to be placed in front of the centre shed. Rob asked that they agree to him hiring a man to live on site, he knew the man he felt would fit the job and proposed to convert the shed nearest to Jensen lane for him and his wife to live in. He had arranged that Harry Atkins and his wife Eve, would come in two days time for an interview.

Harry had been a sergeant in France, in fact Rob said his best sergeant, so Rob knew him very well but felt it necessary that his wife should come so she could view the ex-army hut that would be their home. Rob had some trouble finding Harry, demobbed almost a year now, Rob had traced him to an address in a rather seedy part of the Capital, at this time Harry was out of work and living in one room with Eve's mother. Harry and Eve's reaction to Rob's letter was to say they would accept any job and particularly if living quarters were available. Explaining that their situation was desperate, Eve had become pregnant, as had thousands of others, as soon as Harry had returned from France, they now had a five month old daughter and were living in difficult conditions, that is not too say Eve's mother was unkind to them, indeed she obviously loved them as a family, especially Daughter Kate. Living in such confined quarters brought many problems, both Harry and Eve knew she must not get pregnant again, in such a difficult place it would be impossible to carry on, not only for space but the sheer drudgery of taking a pram up and down the stairs.

Rob had decided on that particular hut as a home for them because he could see it must have been a mess hut of some kind, having a centre kitchen with a large square room on either side of it. By this time Jensen Estates had cleared the army huts from the main site, taking four to re-erect on home farm and had offered the others to anyone who would dismantle them and remove them within two weeks, so now the army was expected any day to clear the roads.

The granary on Johnsons farm was almost full of threshed corn, mostly wheat and both Joe and Tom were keen to see it sold, both being certain the price would soon fall substantially. Although a grateful Government had proclaimed that the British farmer, who had helped feed the nation so well during the war, should never again sink to the levels of poverty experienced in the past. Visiting two of the local corn merchants with samples of wheat, they found prices offered were about seven and a half per cent down on those offered after the harvest, where normally they might have been expected to rise slightly at this time of the year. After discussing it at some length, both Joe and Tom decided to sell, going back to the merchant, Joe asked when he could collect the wheat. The merchant told them he expected Johnsons farm to deliver it to the station, not at that price Joe told him, but agreed to set two men to help load it onto the merchants lorry, so that was the agreed deal. In fact those tons of wheat were the last ones sold from Johnsons farm at a good profit for almost twenty years, many more acres of wheat would, of course, be grown on the farm during those years but returns were destined to be meagre. At least this crop brought a substantial amount of money, so once again the investment fund at the bank could be increased. Rob and Jenny were both at the garage awaiting the arrival of Harry Atkins and Eve, his wife, they were due on the ten o'clock train from London and Jenny had suggested Rob and herself should meet the train. Rob disagreed, telling her that Harry would not expect an ex-Captain to meet an ex- Sergeant and that a walk through the town might help to relax them, and show them a different view of life here to the one that they must be so used to and perhaps had come to hate, in London. Eventually they saw two people approaching, now we will go and meet them, Rob said, as Rob and Jenny came out of the garage, Harry came to Rob, saluted and addressed him with the familiar term Captain. Afterwards, sitting in the office Rob laughed and told him to forget the army, saying both he and Jenny had an equal interest in the garage which made them equal as bosses, but both Harry and Eve must use their christian names, as all other employees did.

Rob then went on to explain the situation on offer, which he considered Harry ideal to fill, Knowing he was tough and honest, thus reliable enough to work and run the new establishment on the trunk road. Jenny explained they were sorry that the accommodation on offer was only an army hut, but it was essential that someone must live on the site for the sake of security, at the moment funds did not allow the building of a new house. "What exactly do you expect of me", Harry asked, "Oh almost everything at first, serve petrol, look after customers, keep the place tidy and be as security conscious as possible when the place is closed", Rob told him. As a long term plan we hope to run a tea room and lorry repair shop on those premises.

Now I think we should go and look at the premises, because they are not very attractive for a lady to live in as yet, although we will spend some money on them and at least they seem snug and dry. Rob and Jenny took them in the car, through Jensen village where they were shown the village shop, then into the new site. As they sat in the car with the trunk road at their back, Rob explained the centre building was to have two petrol pumps in front of it and also act as a simple store, at the rear it was intended eventually a workshop would be made. The building on the right would be the living one and that on the left would be a tea room for motorists and a cafe for lorry drivers. "You have it well planned Cap-Rob", Harry told him, it looks quite attractive to me, even in January, well come and see the living accommodation Jenny said.

They entered at the front, through a door with a window each side of it and another one overlooking Jensen lane, a big room with a substantial stove in its centre, sound in essence but badly in need of decoration. Passing through to the kitchen they saw a large cooking range, with oven and hot plate, many cupboards and two sinks each with a draining board and a water tap to each one, again the room seemed quite sound but in need of decoration and the stove was rusty. The back room, almost as big as the front one, except that right at the back was a small room with a toilet. Rob then explained he would employ a local handyman to partition the rear room into three bedrooms, with a passage giving access to the toilet and back door. Jenny asked Eve if she thought they could settle here, because it may be some years before money allowed a new house to be built.

"Oh I cannot wait to come", Eve replied, " after living as we do now and having to share a toilet and kitchen, carry kate upstairs and down every time I want to go out, this will be heaven, I wish we could come tomorrow. Harry said he could do the decorating, but had no money to buy materials unless ob could pay a weeks wages in advance, Rob said they could do better than that, if he was going to take the job, the garage would buy the decorating materials and pay one weeks wages for Harry to work solely on the house. They would find a half ton of coal to set the fires going and he would arrange for Harry to take firewood from Johnsons farm as a supplementary fuel. On the way back to the garage they called on Johnsons farm, so that Harry and Eve could be introduced to Ma. and Jane, Joe was also there, it being midday. Joe volunteered to take a load of firewood and deposit it by the back door. Jenny then took them home for a cold lunch she had prepared, during which the final details of employment were settled, Eve was asked if she could eventually become involved in the tea room venture, to which she answered yes, explaining whilst

Harry was in France she had worked in a workmens cafe. Finally when all the details were settled they returned to the garage, when do you want me to start harry asked, as soon as you like Rob said but it may take a few days before I can get the back room partitioned. "Oh please say soon, I shall never settle in that back room again after seeing this fine place", Eve told them. Being introduced to the garage staff, Rob asked Bertie, the foreman, if he felt able to collect the Atkin's things the day after tomorrow, yes he replied, so it was settled, the new place on the trunk road had its first staff.

The Harvest dinner was only a day away, a rush of cooking and baking was underway, with Gil and Merri helping, Joe had obtained supplies of Wine and even some Champagne from the London Dairy, the usual barrel of beer was already in place in the village hall, resting before being broached.

The next evening promptly at seven the employees of the three farms and the garage sat down to a plentiful Dinner of hot soup, Prime Beef and vegetables, plus large portions of Johnsons Kitchen fruit pies and custard to follow, even the vicars wife seemed satisfied. Ma. as usual thanked everyone for the efforts made over the last year and looked forward to an equally good 1920, meantime Joe and Tom had filled each champagne glass for a toast to success and many good years to come. With all traces of the meal cleared away, a small band came to lead the dancing and the company took places at small tables set around the walls.

As was usual the barrel of beer was open to all, whilst bottles of wine were available for those who preferred it, a considerable amount of pie was left over and this was placed on a table near the beer barrel so people could help them selves during the evening. Jane watched the vicars wife take two pieces and a glass of wine, I will teach her a lesson Jane thought, at that moment Gil and Merri arrived at the table carrying two newly filled glasses of wine, just watch how much you two drink, Jane reminded them, we don't want any disgraceful behaviour at the end, anyway how much have you already had, "Oh I think two glasses Merri told her, but you should see Pip, she is already gigly and unsteady". Tom on his third glass of beer asked his Dad how he managed to drink so much, Ah Tom, Joe replied there is a secret, you have seen I am always circulating from table to table, I always arrive with a full glass, talk, sit down, take a sip or two and then pass on, but in doing so I top up my glass, probably with only a spoonful or two, it is doubtful if I drink two glasses all night. As Joe came to the table where Jane was sitting, with his glass full as usual, Jane asked him if there was any Champagne left, "yes he told her", "get me a bottle, you can open it easier than I can". With her glass filled Jane walked over to the table where the rev. Williams and his wife were sitting, asked how they were enjoying the Johnsons farm supper, both agreed it was a wonderful affair. "Have some Champagne", Jane asked, but the Rev. Williams declined saying he had finished the one glass of beer he allowed himself, Jane noticed Judith cleared her glass of the wine she had collected with the apple pie and as Jane turned to her, she signified she would fancy a glass.

Sitting down, Jane put the bottle on the table, chatted for a moment and suddenly excused herself, passing over to he mothers table, but leaving the champagne bottle, almost full, behind. Later as Joe came to sit a moment with Jane, he enquired where her champagne had gone, surely you have not drunk it all, "Oh no I left it with Judith aiming to teach her not to be so greedy", Jane told him, Joe laughed, noting the bottle was already half empty. As the night drew to a close Bertie was obviously having trouble getting Pip away, Jane walked over and grabbing her arm, helped Bertie get her into the car. The event came to an end, with people thanking Jane and Joe for a wonderful evening, Ma. had left some time ago, The Rev. Williams came to thank them, it was noticeable that Judith was very quiet having her eyes closed and her husband holding her from collapsing. Jane discreetly watched them go towards the vicarage, luckily it was only just the other side of the church, but Judith obviously could not make it, putting her arms round his neck she kissed him and collapsed, the vicar held her and picked her off the ground, the last thing Jane saw of them was as they rounded the corner of the church on the way home. Turning back to the hall she looked at the debris and decided it was not too bad to leave until tomorrow, locking the door she walked with Joe back to Johnsons farm, catching up with the girls and their husbands on the way. Both girls a little unsteady on their feet but able to walk, the husbands very definitely unsteady. The four young people climbed unsteadily up the stairs whilst Joe locked the back door and put out the lights, Joining Jane in their bedroom he undressed and slipped between the covers, Jane immediately kissed him, afterwards Joe said "you seem affectionate tonight", "yes I am and it is not drink, I have never come home so sober after our annual dinner", Joe leant over and kissed her, gently massaging her breasts and the other tender and secret places he knew she enjoyed, eventually Jane became so demanding that Joe allowed himself to enter her but with periodic withdrawals made their love last until neither could wait any longer and their evening finished in a splendid explosion of amorous passion. Later lying relaxed and drowsy, Joe smiling asked her what made her so passionate, "Oh I don't know, maybe just watching the children go unsteadily to bed", Jane told him, saying she could well remember going upstairs, perhaps in an even worse state than Merri and Gil, "you know Joe the babies will soon be four months old and neither girl has been breast feeding for nearly two months now and Meg tells me they have not been to see her for any more protectives, so perhaps they are not bothering about having another baby, any way I don't suppose they are bothered tonight", Jane said sleepily.

The next morning Frank left early but Gil and Merri agreed to help Jane clear up the village hall, before they left to do that, Jane asked them if they had decided not to worry about having another baby, telling them she knew from Meg they were not taking any precautions that might avoid that situation. Merri looked at Jane, telling her neither of them had a monthly period yet so why use a protector, Jane looked at them both saying I think you are taking a risk, I think you can be caught for a baby without having a period, but I am not sure. Both girls looked at Jane in surprise, but no one told us, Merri said, well Jane told them I only found out from Meg yesterday that you had not been to obtain any more protectors and I think you are taking quite a big risk of having another baby very soon, that is quite alright if you want another to complete your families quickly but you must decide and do it soon. Well I certainly was not taking care last night Merri told her, nor I ,Gil said Frank and I had a wonderful time, I guess we shall have to use a protector all the time now

That night in the office they discussed what crops to grow and whether to concentrate on milk or meat, Joe was certain that Hard Canadian and American wheat would soon be arriving, but they had already planted the normal acreage of winter wheat. Milk seemed to be a good product to produce, after all as Joe said, it was not easy to import milk, so in the end they decided to leave things as they were for 1920 and see what changes in demand peace time might bring. Tom suggested that the guaranteed prices, a basic below which they would not be allowed to fall, in his opinion would prove too expensive for the government to maintain, this could bring big problems to the farming industry in the not too far distant future. Tom reminded them that the case of Harry Atkins was now quite common, the war production had ceased, most of the women factory workers were not now needed and thousands of men returning home from the forces could not find work. Tom felt that the government of whatever party would spend money, if it had any, om the unemployment problem to gain votes from hundreds of thousands, rather than on a smaller number of farmers. Joe agreed and said how pleased he was that they had kept up so well with mechanising the farm, also what a good thing they had put on one side money with the bank, it may well be needed yet. But just one thing he now thought they should do was to get an estimate for the work on the farmhouse so the work could be started as soon as the sewer was being laid down the main street. By getting an estimate now he felt the amount of money could be put on one side from the wheat money and the rest put to the reserve fund.

Ted Rudge had spoken to Joe to enquire if Johnsons farm

would release Bill Worsley back to the estate, so he could resume his position as under gamekeeper, that was of course if Bill agreed. Ted had told Joe his Lordship was planning to build three new cottages and one could be made available for Bill, but it may be six months or so before they were ready. They all agreed that Bill would be missed on the farm but in view of what they had been speaking about maybe the loss of one farm worker may be a good thing in the long run, joe said he would speak to Bill the next day.

Bertie delivered Harry and Eve to their new home, Jenny and Jane had, during the morning, swept out the living room and kitchen and lit the fires in both rooms. So when the lorry arrived with Harry, Eve and Kate plus their belongings the place was reasonably warm, the furniture set out around the centre stove and the bed put up, for now, in the living room and a cup of tea made ready, they began to feel at home. Just before dark, Rob and Jenny arrived, both to be sure the Atkins were as comfortable as possible and to say they would collect them and visit the paint and wallpaper shop the next morning. They were able to tell Harry and Eve that the carpenter would come tomorrow to start and partition the back room, the cold wind on the new site was causing Rob to cough quite heavily and so Jenny hurried him home to use the inhaler that Joe provided. By the end of January the Atkins were settled in, warm and snug, Joe had shown Harry what wood he could take from the spinney and provided a horse and cart for him to carry it home. Bertie was learning Harry to drive and the petrol company was installing the two petrol pumps and a large sign as promised.

The aftermath of the farm dinner was becoming obvious,

Pip came to see Jenny to tell her she was almost certain she was having a baby, Judith the vicars wife told Jane she must have conceived the night of the dinner, but could not remember just what had happened, it must have been the champagne she said,"well perhaps you were a little greedy with it", Jane said. The biggest surprise was that Jill Worsley had to tell them she would soon have to stop work, she was amazed by it all, but felt sure she was pregnant, believing it must be as a result of some Christmas celebrations.

Most serious of all, at least to Merri, was that Gil rang one afternoon to tell her she was sure she had suffered morning sickness that day. Merri discussed this with Jane, saying she was worried that if Gil was again pregnant, then it was likely she herself was. Jane smiled at her, telling her they would be so happy if she was, after all it was better to have babies early in marriage, "I know, but I feel so silly being caught for another baby so soon after Jay, it looks as if I cannot control my feelings", said Merri, "well can you?", asked Jane, "no and it begins to seem as if Tom cannot either". A week later two anxious wife's visited the doctor, Gil was now certain she was pregnant and Merri, feeling a tenderness around the nipples of her breasts felt almost as certain as Gil. After a thorough examination of them both the doctor decided they would probably have August babies, but since neither girl had any idea when they had conceived he emphasised that was only an estimate.

Ellenor was of course overjoyed, as really was Jane, but a little concerned that Merri was not too pleased. Gil and Frank had now accepted the situation with good grace, but Merri was still a little resentful, because she now realised that driving the tractor in the corn harvest, as she had promised herself, was now going to be impossible. Tom did not make matters any better, he kept saying he had warned her to be more careful, but Merri soon told him she had not noticed him being so very careful. But that night in their bedroom Merri very soon kissed him and as they lay naked in bed, Tom found, as ever, that he could not deny an aroused and demanding Merri, "Oh Tom we need not worry now, but it is next September that worries me", she told him.

Halfway through February an army marque arrived on the old army camp, Joe was soon there to see who was in charge, finding a sergeant, a corporal and six men, joe soon asked the sergeant what he was going to do with the rubble from the roads he was there to take up. "I was planning to cart it over the road and fill the low lying ground by the sewage farm", he told Joe, it is going to be hard work breaking up that road Joe said, have you some more men coming, another ten and two lorries Joe was told. Can we strike a deal, that I will provide Eggs bacon and ham, all home produced, if you will arrange for your men to break the old surface fairly small and spread it on our site across the road, the man who lives there will show you where. Eventually the new garage had a good road to the petrol pumps, a large car park and a road round to the rear of the central building ready to start an emergency workshop. By the end of March the army had left and Harry had spent hours rolling the new roadway and car park with one of the old Mogul tractors, whose fairly flat wheels proved ideal for the job.

The threshing machine had been put away, having finished its winter programme, Jil had worked until it had finished, going home to prepare for the birth of her new baby, but assuring them that she wanted to continue working on the set as soon as possible after the birth, hoping Jane Knowles would look after it as she looked after the others. The days drew out and although the weather was catchy, warm sunshine, then clouds might race across the sky and for af few minutes a heavy shower would fall, only to be replaced with sunshine again. The spring work went well, in spite of this catchy weather, the field workers, hoeing root crops, enjoying birdsong and even the angry squawking, as small birds squabbled over whose wife it was, or whose nest it may be.

Bill Worsley had elected to return to his first love of being a gamekeeper, his wife Jill now showing clear signs of the new life within her, was happy in the Johnsons farm cottage, she could still potter in the garden and enjoy the fresh air and exercise. The new cottages on the estate were only just started and so would not be ready until the autumn. Billy and Harry Downs had put the Fordson tractors in the shed and were now busy horse hoeing the root crops, of which Joe and Tom had decided to increase the acreage, particularly of potatoes. The Fordson tractors were later brought out to pull the mowing machines to start the hay harvest, this was a very busy time with the roots to finish hoeing and the hay crop to gather.

CHAPTER THREE

Purse strings begin to tighten

This year of 1920 saw no labour shortage, as England began to come to grips with the peace, unemployment began to rise, farm crops showed some sign of easing in price, but Johnsons farm looking forward to a good and heavy harvest seemed to be in as good a position as it might be possible to be. Imported wheat prices had halved the price of english wheat, just as Joe and Tom had anticipated, but this years crop looked good and they hoped that it may, at least break even. The sewer was being laid through Jensen village and Johnsons farm was being modernised, the cost was higher than anticipated, but as Joe told them, "if we don't do it now we may have to wait years, after this expense we must run a fairly strong economy campaign". The harvest went well, but a little slower than other years due to the missing members of the labour force, in the second week in September both Merri and Gil gave birth, Gil first with a daughter, Ellenor Jane and two days later Merri provided the family with a son, Joseph William. It goes without saying that everyone was so pleased, no regrets from the two new mothers now, about how quickly they had started their second babies, just joy and a happy feeling it was all over.

As soon as the corn harvest was finished the root harvest began, harvesting roots is always a hard and often wet experience. Having started the root harvest a little early, due to the shortage of help it went well, at first, the weather being kind, potatoes came first and Jane was pressed into service ferrying cart loads from the field to the clamp in the stackyard, Joe spent most of his time tidying up the clamp and covering them over to keep out the winter frost he well knew would eventually come. Tom was driving the lorry, delivering milk and produce, in place of Merri who was longing to get back to work, although she felt able to do so, Jane had persuaded her to wait just a little longer so as not to distort the feeding times of Will, as everyone now called him. Jill Worsleys baby, Jackson, was born at the end of September and she was looking forward to renewing her duties on the threshing machine, which had not yet been brought out of storage. A little later there was joy at the garage when Pip presented Bertie with a son, Herbert John, and Judith Williams also had a son, to be called Luke. So now the excitement of new babies in 1920 was over and Joe was left wondering what the next few years might bring, he was not anticipating an easy time. Billy and Harry Downs were ploughing with the two Fordson tractors so once again Joe and Tom had to spend part of their Sunday morning servicing them, but the ploughing was going well and they hoped to have some wheat planted in a few weeks time. The village ladies had done stirling work lifting the potatoes, but it became more and more obvious that they could not handle the large acreage of mangolds and swedes that lay ahead, particularly now the weather was becoming colder and the days shorter, but several local men who had been laid off came looking for work, this eased the problem and the root harvest accelerated, Jane again ferrying loads of roots to the clamp whilst Joe kept it in order and well covered.

Gil and Merri were now almost finished breast feeding and were trying hard to control their feelings for Frank and Tom, but not finding it easy, both young mothers desperate not to get caught for another baby. Gil was now helping Ellenor with the business accounts as well as the house work, a local girl had been hired to look after the two babies, James and Jane. With Gil now reasonably proficient at the accounts Frank sen. And Ellenor decided to take a weeks holiday, never having had one since their honeymoon, the summer and autumn rush had quietened down a little and that was the spur for them to arrange a holiday before the spring rush of machinery sales started. Having enjoyed their week away they came back full of praise for the hotel they had selected on the south coast and talked Gil and Frank into making a booking for the next May, when they all expected the weather to be better.

Gil and Frank were now calculating the period of each month when they must use the protectors, still supplied by Meg, with great care, Gil being terrified of becoming pregnant again. They were finding the protectors more usable now since they had been told to use butter as a lubricant, but even so Gil was still apprehensive one might fail at a vital time, but Frank was unconcerned, telling her it was most unlikely and if it did fail, maybe fate intended that to happen. Merri, just as anxious as Gil, but perhaps with a slightly more happy go lucky personality was, nevertheless, trying hard to make the protectors work, it was not an easy time for either wife.

It was now becoming more and more evident that farming was not going to have an easy time, just as Tom had predicted, the government panicked and replaced the assurance given to farmers that never again would they be abandoned to their fate, with a much more open statement that the farmers could not rely on an open purse. The population at large must be given the advantage of low world food prices of all kinds, but the government felt that by mechanising their farms they would still make a reliable and steady living, the government assured farmers it would watch the situation carefully and take any action necessary. At an evening meeting in the study, this statement was taken to mean"look out for yourselves", both Joe and Tom believed Johnsons farm was in as strong a position as any farm in the locality, but neither could suggest one product to specialise in to keep the farm solvent. Agreeing that they could only go on as before and produce the diversity of crops they were accustomed to produce.

They all agreed costs must be cut, Joe had never taken on more women workers than the original six, several had enquired, now factory and war work was at an end, but he declined their offers. Bill Worsley was no longer being paid by Johnsons farm and right out of the blue Tim Kealy's brother, who had worked with Tim ever since Johnsons farm had taken over Riverside, decided to leave, having a better paid job in Cambridge offered to hin by the meat processing factory which took part of the output of pigs from Riverside farm. Tim and Meg's two daughters, both strapping country girls were to be paid another one pound per week to replace him. The general consensus of opinion was that Johnsons farm would find it hard going, with such a depleted labour force, but as Tom pointed out there was likely to be a bigger surplus of labour in the area, so perhaps they could hire some casual labour if needed.

Joe asked the question, "are we to keep Walter the German ex prisoner of war on our books or must he make way for an ex soldier", Tom pointed out that Walter was an ex soldier, yes Joe told him but from the German side, Tom thought that if the demand for rabbits kept up next year Walter, who was first class at his job, should be asked to catch more rabbits, by spending more time at the job and taking over the warrens vacated by Bill Worsley and his wife Jill. This would mean Walter might become self sustaining as far as wages went and still be able to help on the farm for a few hours each day. After such a long discussion it was quite late as they retired to bed, it was evident both children were asleep in the nursery and Jane Knowles had no light under her door in the next room to the children. Merri decided to forego her nightly visit to them, leaving all in peace with no risk of awakening them.

In their own room they undressed in silence, drawing the curtains back to look out over a cold but moonlit countryside, Merri saying " you know Tom we are so lucky to have such a wonderful life in spite of the problems we have been speaking of tonight", "yes I know, Tom told her but are you going to stand there looking out of the window for ever on such a cold night". Climbing into bed Merri was snuggled up to him, ten minutes later they were as warm as toast, Merri having her nightie around her neck, whilst Tom had skilfully stripped off his nightshirt, he turned to kiss her, raising himself on one elbow, the better to reach her willing lips. You know he told her, I realise how terrible it must be to be unemployed, short of money and to be frightened to touch your wife in case you give her another mouth to feed. "Well at least we are not that bad off, but don't get carried away, we may be able to afford another baby but we certainly are not going to start one tonight, we played long enough last night and I have not had time to go and see Meg today, so last night will have to last you until tomorrow"."Oh that is alright, I can wait but we can still kiss and cuddle a little", said Tom, Merri left him in no doubt that was all they could do tonight.

After a time of affectionate kissing Tom slid his arm under her shoulders and cupped one of her breasts in his other hand, now their lips met at a better angle and as Tom felt her breasts, and particularly the nipples harden, he gently opened her lips with his tongue and began to explore the inner parts of her mouth. With a gasp of pleasure Merri slid her tongue into his mouth, he sensed he wriggling slightly and whilst this passionate behaviour was continued Tom gently moved his hand from her breast, tracing a line down her flat stomach and coming to rest on her thigh, just above the knee. Merri reacted quickly, putting her arms from loosely around his body she put them round his neck and pulled his face and lips closer than ever to her own, then gently opened her legs as Tom slid his hand up the inside of a warm and willing thigh, until he met the exciting place, now wide open to him, that they both knew so well. "Oh Tom I love you so much but do be careful, it must be dangerous tonight, the way I feel", "I love you Merri, just let me lie over you, but not go inside", now so warm and damp, Merri had great difficulty recognising just where Tom was. He brought his lips and tongue to hers again and played with the hard and erect nipple on her left breast, as he again explored her mouth with his tongue, he felt Merri open her legs wider and push herself up to him, he knew instantly that he was deep inside her. Struggling slightly he withdrew and lay quiet, was that nice he asked her, " wonderful but not properly finished", Merri replied " Ah but we cannot finish it tonight", Tom told her," well just one more time then", Merri said. As they lay quiet for a minute, Merri told Tom to be so careful, but I do want you one more time. Tom with his hand exploring the inside of her thighs, told her he had never seen her so aroused, Merri laughed telling him it was his fault for being such a wonderful husband. Perhaps we should stop now Tom suggested, I am so aroused myself, it will be so very much more difficult to stop next time, well don't go in just lie there and kiss me then we will go to sleep, but I must have just one more touch. Merri straightened her legs down the bed with her thighs clamped together, Tom gently astride her felt her warm hard breasts on his chest, as their lips met again Tom felt Merri relax her thighs and he slipped between them. They lay for a short time, Merri with her arms round Tom's waist and his lips and tongue caressing her mouth, she wriggled a little and Tom felt himself slip into a hot cavern. Careful he said, lie still a minute, as they continued to kiss Merri suddenly put her arms around Tom's buttocks and arched her back, pulling on his buttocks with surprising strength. Tom realised he was about to explode, Merri released her grip slightly and as he began to withdraw, she again pulled him into her, lips in contact, tongues engaged and hard nipples rubbing his chest, Tom knew it was too late to worry. After a few moments he moved inside again and Merri responded, later completely satisfied they lay together in one anothers arms. Looking into her eyes in the moonlight Tom asked why she had not allowed him to withdraw, a smiling Merri told him he must ask mother nature that question, Merri told him she just could not stop. The next morning Merri, not quite so happy now, said to him"well I guess we shall have to put up with three babies in three years, I don't think I will go and visit Meg now, i guess there is no need".

The new garage site on the trunk road was now open, but

only for petrol, the tea room and drivers cafe was being prepared, a kitchen made in the centre of the building with a tea room at the front and the drivers cafe to the rear. Harry had found that the afternoons were much less busy on the petrol pumps and had learned Eve to dispense petrol, this left Harry free to carry on with the decorating of the food places during the afternoons. Meantime Rob had been a regular visitor, but perhaps because of this, he was now confined to bed, yet again, with breathing problems. Jenny now came most afternoons and on one visit decided they should soon open to the many drivers who used the trunk road. Discussing with Eve, they decided 8am to 6pm.would be acceptable hours and Jenny left to purchase utensils, tables, chairs and linen cloths for the tea room. Two days later they were delivered and the following Monday two ladies from Jensen village arrived to prepare for the opening on the next day. One of the ladies had a Daughter who had agreed to prepare pies and cakes for the tea room, whilst hot food for the lorry drivers cafe would be prepared on site. By this time a telephone had been installed and already had been used by Harry to call the garage, in Little Staunton out to repair two punctures and one breakdown. By the end of the first week, a small profit had been produced and Rob, now back at work was pleased with the result.

The garage was still not getting sufficient supplies of vehicles, they had a small waiting list, but had two tractors in stock. Merri was due to take one to a farm about ten miles away and it was hoped that it would stay on the farm if the demonstration went well, the car salesman, who had some knowledge of tractors was to accompany her. On the morning of the demonstration, Tom took the supplies to the station and the dairy, dropping Merri off at the garage. She looked so smart in the blue and white overalls, marked with the word Fordson across her shoulders, Rob came out to see the tractor loaded, which Merri did easily, after all she had now done five demonstrations over the two years, when she was able, babies permitting. A plough, well prepared with shiny earth wearing parts had been delivered to the farm the previous day by one of the garage mechanics. The salesman led the way in his car and Merri followed with the lorry and tractor. At the farm, the farmer and his son came to look and whilst they talked with the salesman Merri pulled out the short, light, loading ramps, started the tractor and backed it off the lorry.

She walked over to the men, bidding them good morning, asked where the plough was, looking at Merri the farmer said "in the stackyard, through that gate", Merri soon climbed on to the tractor and moved it into the stackyard, when the men arrived she already had the plough hooked to the tractor and was tying the trip rope, which operated the plough lift gear, to the tractor seat. "Where do we plough", asked Merri, "Joe here, indicating the son, opened a piece with the horses yesterday, over in that field, it is dry but heavy land and I want the tractor to plough as deep as the horses", the farmer told the salesman. Right Merri the salesman told her " go and get started we will walk across", "but aren't you going to drive the tractor", the farmer asked, he was left in no doubt that Merri was the demonstrator and that the salesman had never ploughed.

"I hope she does not make a mess of our field", the farmer said, "don't worry, the salesman replied, she is a good operator and might even improve on the work already started", the farmer soon told the salesman he did not think that would be so, because his son was a good ploughman. Merri arrived at the piece of ploughing, stepped off the tractor and proceeded to measure the depth at which Joe had ploughed the day before. "It varies from four and a half to five inches, but I expect we can go a bit deeper than that, but not too much or we may be into clay, I will do a couple of rounds to see and straighten the furrows, then I will stop and see what you think". After two rounds Merri had almost got the furrows straight and was ploughing six inches deep, "I could go deeper still but it will bring up too much clay, if you plough six inches this year perhaps you can go six and a half next year", an amazed farmer was told. After another two rounds, with straight furrows and even work, Merri stopped again and asked if one of the farm men wanted to try the outfit, "Joe you wanted a tractor, now is the time to see if you still do so", said the farmer, Joe climbed gingerly on to the seat and as Merri stood on the plough drawbar, giving instructions, they started off across the field.

After three rounds Merri stepped off the, telling Joe to try a round himself. Half an hour later the farmer stopped Joe to ask what he thought about it, " Oh dad its wonderful, I know we should buy it". "Well we will go and have a drink in the kitchen and discuss it", the farmer said. Joe drove the tractor to the farm, Merri showed him how to stop it, so it would be easy to start and they all adjourned to the farm kitchen for a cup of tea and a home made scone. " Well I never expected to see a slip of a girl plough better, faster and deeper than our heavy horses", the farmer told them, after some discussion a price was agreed, Joe laughingly said he hoped the girl came along with the tractor, Merri told him she did not know what her husband and two children might have to say about that.

Afterwards Merri and Joe returned to the tractor and Merri showed Joe how to start it and where to put the petrol for starting, kerosene for running and how to check the oil levels, she insisted he greased all grease points as well as checking oil levels twice each day. Joe started the tractor and carried on ploughing, Merri watched for a while and then returned to the farm, the salesman had left, with a cheque, leaving an instruction book on the tractor at the farm. Merri loaded the ramps on the lorry and was just climbing into the cab when the farmer came, he thanked her for showing off the tractor so well and spending time with Joe, all part of the job she assured him, telling him to be sure and contact them if Joe found anything he did not understand. Returning to the garage Merri parked the lorry and found Pip cleaning a new car, now with baby in a carriage, Merri told her she was going to walk over to see Gil and then perhaps Pip would drive her home.

Merri found Gil clearing up the dinner pots, Ellenor had gone to the office and the children were being looked after by the nursemaid, sitting with a cup of tea, Merri asked Gil how her love life was progressing, just a bit fraught, Gil told her, Frank is very good but always looking to take a risk and I am determined not to be caught for another baby for a long time yet. Anyway how are you managing, Merri told her how she had behaved with Tom and was now certain she was again having a baby, at least we are enjoying the freedom, Merri told her, we have never used a protector for more than a week now.

The winter ploughing on Johnsons farm was not yet finished but the ground was too wet to carry on, just at present, in the meantime the Christmas rush was starting and again all staff were set to work doing the preparation work, perhaps not quite as heavy a demand this year as last but it still put considerable pressure on the farm. One afternoon a smiling Merri whispered to Tom that she now knew they were not going to have another baby, and he had better get his mind into a safety mode for the future. After Christmas the weather being a bit drier the tractors had started ploughing again, the 1921 farm supper came around and this year there were no unexpected pregnancies, both Gil and Merri were very careful indeed how much the drank.

On the farm a concentrated effort was being made to empty the manure yard and the fold yards, this was done by again using Jane as a ferry driver whilst two people in the field spread the manure and two at the farm loaded the carts. When all the fields had been spread that needed spreading two large heaps were made in the positions where they would be needed for application after the next harvest. By mid February the spring work was underway, some of the fields where the manure had been spread were ploughed quite deeply, partly to bury the manure and partly to leave a good depth of soil ready to prepare for the root crops, the oats and barley were set, the mangolds, turnips and potatoes followed. The threshing machine finished last harvests corn and the granary was fuller than Joe could remember it being in late spring, he felt sure no extra feed would be needed to buy during the summer.

Walter, the ex German prisoner of war was now officially walking out with Elizabeth Knowles, daughter of Jim and Jessie Knowles who lived on Moorside farm and he showed no sign of wishing to return to Germany, he was, of course free to do so now, he explained that his position before the war, as assistant woodsman to his Father, would not give him the standard of life he had in England. In any case he did not feel able to leave Elizabeth and he certainly could not ask her to leave England and go to a very impoverished Germany, she could not yet speak much German either, although Walter was slowly teaching her his language.

The end of April and early May brought a scene Joe loved to watch, six or eight people working across a field of roots with their hoes, singling the turnips and mangolds, that is cutting out almost all the newly grown plants, but leaving just one strong plant every six inches. This was hard work, repetitious and back breaking, it was likely to take a month to complete and although much of the weather at this time of year was mild, there were still days almost wintery with cold squalls of wind and heavy showers. Of course there were others when the spring sunshine burned the workers almost ebony as the sun anticipated the hot days of summer yet to come. Joe and Tom took a hoe each to add two more hands to this work, as often as they could, Joe telling Tom a farmer must not only show his workers that he could do the jobs himself but needed the skills to appreciate what his workers may try to tell him and to evaluate if they were trying to pull the wool over his eyes in some way.

One evening Jo, daughter of Josie, whose husband Jake had been one of the early casualties in France during the war asked her mother if she could talk with her. It seemed John Deane had been walking her home from events in the village hall and had asked Jo if she would walk out with him. Jo was sufficiently uncertain of her feelings for him, to make her seek the advice of her mother and anyway did her mother feel comfortable if Jo was to spend some evenings walking out with John. After all Jo had very rarely been away from Josie and Jake, now a fine five year old, since he had been born, in that tragic time just after Jake had been killed in France. Josie thought for a moment and then told Jo the time was coming when she must at least, think about a life away from her and Jake, Josie had always felt this time must come and realised a pretty and attractive daughter, such as Jo was, would inevitably attract young men. Josie replied, of course she must walk out with John or how would she know what her feeling for him were, but Josie did emphasise to walk out, not to "walk the ricks" and then to have to face the almost inevitable ending, of becoming pregnant. "Oh mother how could you think I would do a thing like that, before I ws married", well Josie told her, thousands have and I thought it worth mentioning.

Tom and Merri at last seemed to have their love life organised, they both used and respected the protectors supplied by Meg, but of course loved the days when Merri made the decision that they need not use one to-night.

At the garage on the trunk road Harry and Eve and even little Kate had settled well, the tea room and cafe were making a steady profit, Eve acting as manageress, although that was rather a grand title for a lady who both looked after her daughter Kate and served in the tea room, as well as keeping the accounts. Harry had set flowers around the three ex army huts and also whitened them, in addition he was now setting an area of the car park with kerb stones to make a segregated parking area for the many private cars that now called.

Working late on this project one evening in late April, he came into the kitchen asking Eve if there was enough hot water in the stove for a bath, Eve told him yes and she also would have one and would fill the bath if Harry would carry it in for her. The bath hung by the back door and Harry soon had it carried into the kitchen and stood on the rug in front of the large army range, that not only heated the water but also did the cooking and warmed the kitchen to a cosy temperature, particularly now the curtains were drawn as it was already dark outside. With large towels spread out on the floor, one each side the bath and a half full bath of wonderful warm water, Eve was soon standing naked, "you go first, I am much dirtier than you", Harry told her. Eve stepped into the bath and gingerly sat down in the rather too warm water, Harry meantime took off his clothes and came to wash Eve's back, not forgetting to give her an affectionate kiss as he did so. It was soon obvious that one kiss was not enough, kissing her gently he was soon washing her all over whilst Eve clung to him with her arms around his neck and with their lips in contact.

Eventually Eve washed harry's back, still naked and as he climbed from the bath Eve came to him with a lingering and somewhat sexy kiss, "hey remember what you told me last night" Harry said " you cannot be free to make love tonight if you were not last night", Eve laughed at him, telling him she had lost the will to care. As they walked into their bedroom to put on their night clothes, Eve turned to him, his need for her was obvious, she leaned her head backwards and with her arms round his neck kissed him with vigour, Harry responded and they both fell on the bed. Half an hour later they both slept, as naked as the day they were born. First light came and Harry awoke, as his eyes blinked to control the brightening day light, he saw Eve leaning over him with shining eyes and a smile on her lips, "well you took some awakening, did I really tire you so much last night", Eve asked, well I am not tired now Harry told her, good she replied, leaving him in no doubt why she was pleased he was no longer tired.

Late in May Gil and Frank prepared for their trip to the south coast, with luggage packed, the car cleaned and ready Frank asked Gil if he should take some protectors, Gil, with a smile told him no, by sheer chance this was a safe week, but he had better have some ready when they returned home. Just south of London a heavy and constant knocking developed in the car, Frank decided it was the transmission and called in to a garage. The mechanic confirmed it was in the rear axle, the manager thought he could get the repair done the day after tomorrow, they had not time to start it until next day. What to do, that was the question, the garage manager suggested he took them to a nice country hotel nearby, where they could book in for two nights. Then carry on with their journey, this they did, Frank telephoning his father to tell them where they had booked in, because Ellenor, looking after the children, may want to contact Gil. Frank sen. Told him to telephone the hotel on the coast to let them know what had happened and book a few more days there, business was very quiet and it was not necessary for them to hurry back.

In the meantime, on Johnsons farm, Joe and Tom had the Fordson tractors coupled to the mowers ready to start the hay harvest, although that event would most likely be two or three weeks away. Tom meantime had visited Walter at Moorside farm, asking him to start the rabbit snaring season, there being more rabbits than ever. It was no longer an evening and early morning activity, but with six warrens spread over almost 1600 acres it was almost a full time job, but Elizabeth said she would help. The old bucks and pregnant females were buried when they were caught in the snares, only prime rabbits were supplied to the London dairy and the farm shop in Little Staunton. At the end of the first week when rabbits were again available the demand was increasing. Ma. now almost seventy years old, was under pressure not to work so hard in the kitchen, as Joe told her, if she could still cope with the bookkeeping it would be a great help. The situation was made easier when Jill said she would help in the kitchen, if her children could again be looked after along with Merri's, in the nursery, so Jill came to work full time in the farm kitchen. Franks car was repaired but not until three days plus the first two had passed, this was due to a failure of the ring gear, and a three day delay in obtaining another. The hotel on the coast were made aware of this extra delay but told Frank not too worry they would count his seven night stay from the day he arrived.

Eventually Frank and Gil arrived six days later than expected but all was arranged and their holiday started at last, although in truth the country hotel had made them most welcome, it also had a good dining room and wine cellar. The hotel on the coast was just as luxurious as Frank's mum and dad had told them it was, facing the sea their bedroom was so very well appointed, with a separate room containing a toilet, wash basin and large bath. After five days Gil had become used to luxuriating in the bath before they dressed for dinner, this night she was in the bath having a lovely soak, when Frank walked in, completely naked, saying move over darling let me get in with you, Gil soon moved and Frank, putting his arms round her shared a wonderful watery kiss, Gil felt her breasts harden and kissed Frank with some abandon, she had known he was aroused as soon as he had walked into the bathroom, but that was as nothing now, with the effect of warm water on two bodies so much in love. As they wriggled together,

Frank suggested he lie in the bath and Gil sit on him with her legs by his arms, Gil laughing soon accomplished this balancing act and with some trial and error found Frank could enter her, very soon they had some lovely feelings come over them, after a while they both lay down together, later dried and dressed for dinner Gil asked Frank how far he had gone in the bath, "Oh all the way ", he told her, it was wonderful. "Yes I suppose it would be, it was wonderful for me too, but you know we should have been at home three days ago and using the protectors". After some more calculations Gil told him she must be in the time when she might have another baby very easily, she had not thought of this when they were delayed, it had only just come to her how dangerous it may be to make love at this time without a protector. " Well I guess we shall have to stop all this loving until we get home", Frank told her, Gil suggested it would be easier to say than do and in truth she did not think she could stop for three whole days. After a drink in the cocktail bar whilst they studied the menu, Frank asked if she was set on not making love tonight, because surely they should not take wine with their dinner. "Oh I think we will, after the last few days and this afternoons escapade I think it is much too late to bother". Three more wonderful days and they set off for home, but Gil was sue she must be having another baby.

The singling almost finished on Johnsons farm and Harry Downs had half the potato crop earthed up, the hoeing gang were finally going through the root crops, no careful singling to do now, it was quick, if not easy work, Billy was running the horse hoe down each row after the hoeing gang had hand hoed between the plants left six inches apart. Johnsons farm with its tractors and horses had usually found time to lightly cultivate the stubble after the harvest and before the winter ploughing, this was to kill any weed seeds left on the ground, which would chit and start to grow after being disturbed by the cultivator, then they would be killed by the winter ploughing. Even so there were always a few of the more persistent weeds, such as thistles and docks that survived and this was the time, after hoeing and before or during the hay harvest, that the hoeing gang systematically walked through the corn crops pulling out the few specimens found.

The hay harvest called for some good organisation, Janice now the cows were not inside all the time, was free to ride the mower for Merri, Harry Downs drove the second tractor and Elizabeth would ride the mower and later the binder for him, returning to help Walter with the rabbits in the late afternoon or evening. Billy was free to use the horse hoe but his main job was to build the hay and corn stacks. Life went on quietly on the farm, life got harder, profits fell but during 1922 Gil had her third child, courtesy of a broken down motor car, it was a daughter who was named Abigail Jennifer. Eve also had her second baby again a girl Ruby, if Harry was disappointed not to have a son, he did not show it, to Eve he just showed Joy and thanks for a lovely daughter. Eve was soon up and about, with Ruby just three weeks old Eve was again working part time in the Tea room, Jenny protesting Eve should not return so soon but to no avail.

In fact it was Jenny who was overworked, Rob had been taken ill in November, his breathing was more difficult than ever and the doctor warned them he may become a permanent invalid, unless he could leave Little Staunton and go to a drier and clearer climate. This matter was discussed at one of the evening meetings, the doctor had recommended a clinic in Switzerland, this was likely to be costly but all agreed the money must be found, Jenny telling them the garage could afford the cost at present, but there may come a time when it would be more than it could bear. Both Johnsons farm and Gil, the other shareholders in the garage, agreed to contribute the year end dividends they were due to receive in March, towards the cost of Rob's treatment. The doctor set up the visit with the clinic and during February Jenny and Rob set off, taking the boat train to Paris and a direct train to Switzerland, Rob was rigged up with plenty of Joe's inhaler and all they could do was to hope.

It was an easy journey, Rob only having to use the inhaler once, just after leaving Paris. Arriving at the clinic Jenny stayed in the clinics own hotel for four days to see what the doctors assessment of Rob might mean, Rob had been placed on the list of a slim, young looking doctor, although he had white hair, his name Doctor Jurgen. On the afternoon of the third day, Jenny and Rob, now an "in" patient, presented themselves in Doctor Jurgens study. He sat them down and started his analysis of Rob's condition, as they knew, one lung was almost destroyed by the gas Rob had mysteriously breathed during his time in the trenches in France, although there had never been a gas attack confirmed.

Doctor Jurgen had a small hope that he could recover that damaged lung by a small amount, by fluid draining, the other lung, still quite good, but showing signs of taking up some of the gas problem from the first lung, that was Rob's current problem. The Doctor explained a stay of perhaps eight or twelve weeks with intermittent treatment and walks in the crisp dry air, might make a lot of difference to Rob. Particularly if the second lung could be cleared and the first lung perhaps dried off, and if some element of use could be retained. Doctor Jurgens diagnosis was, in the main, reasonably optimistic, he believed the second lung could be recovered and this would enable Rob to lead a normal life, but would need to take care in the damp cold English Winter.

Jenny returned home the next day, Bertie had been in charge of the garage and Jane had spent three hours each day on the accounts, but this could only be a temporary solution. Jenny's son David had been staying with Rob's mother and so the day after Jenny returned and told her family of Doctor Jurgens diagnosis, she drove over to the Graham farm to give them the news and collect David. It had provisionally been arranged with Doctor Jurgens that Jenny would visit Rob in eight weeks time and the Doctor would give her a progress report. It was thus that Jenny found herself in Switzerland once again during May. She had delayed the trip, partly due to seven cars and three lorries being made available by Ford and partly that during Rob's absence Jenny had time to think of the future. Jenny had thought of David eventually taking over the farm, it had come to her how the garage was growing and if David took to the Graham farm, who would inherit the garage.

According to the many letters Jenny received from Rob, he was much improved but agreed that the wonderful treatment and swiss air were working wonders, he told her he could not wait to see her again and hopefully make love to her, something he had not been able to do for almost a year. The thoughts Jenny had experienced and Rob's letters gave Jenny the idea that Switzerland might just be the place to conceive an heir for the garage, thus Jenny had delayed her trip to cover what she considered an opportune time. Jenny took the usual trains, but this time took a sleeping berth on the overnight journey from Paris to Zurich, arriving at the clinic in time for lunch, Jenny was so pleased to find that, although their reunion kisses were long and affectionate, Rob gave no sign of breathlessness. Doctor Jurgen spent a few minutes with them and told them they could live together in the clinic's hotel, because Rob was in a break time from his treatment, but he must spend two hours each morning on the programme of breathing exercises he was undergoing and must keep to his afternoon walks of at least four kilometres.

During lunch Rob told Jenny he would take her that afternoon on one of his favourite walks, it was quite a long way uphill, but if he walked normally and did not rush, it did not affect his breathing and at the end was a wonderful view over a valley. After lunch, Jenny dressed for the walk but whilst doing so Rob came over to her and kissed her, in the loving manner she so well remembered from two years ago. Jenny realised she was already feeling the need for Rob to make love to her, but decided it must wait for to-night, because surely she believed, someone would be looking for them to take the promised daily walk. As they left the hotel, Rob confidently turned uphill and with normal strides kept a steady walking pace, after about forty five minutes the road petered out into a stony path, they were well passed the tree line and just simple outcrops of rock with wonderful patches of green grass were all around them. Rob surprised Jenny with his steady walking pace, he did not seem out of breath but Jenny was, Rob laughed and told her he was now used to the higher altitude whereas Jenny was used to living almost at sea level.

They walked along the stony path, a few butterflies flitting about and frequenting the mass of alpine flowers along with bees and smaller insects, blue sky above and Jenny was already feeling the heat of the sun. Suddenly Rob turned right and after a few yards Jenny found herself overlooking a valley, the view almost took her breath away as she found herself standing on the edge of a sheer drop, hundreds of feet to the valley floor. The path dipped down as it passed along this sheer edge, passing in front of a large outcrop of rock, as she turned Rob was sitting on a ledge almost cut out as a seat, Jenny dropped down beside him struggling for breath, but managing to gasp" goodness it must be me that needs treatment".

Rob put his arms round her saying "Oh Jenny I love you so much, no one will ever know how much I have missed you these long weeks passed". Jenny turned to face him and received a long loving kiss, eventually they broke away, Rob asking how she liked his secret place, telling her he often came to sit here and watch the farmers on the valley floor going about their work. I bring my field glasses up her so I can see better what they are doing, Rob told her, see the distant horse and covered chaise, that is the bread man delivering the afternoon new bread, but I have never been able to make out what else he delivers beside bread, they both stood on the edge of the path watching the tiny figures at work below, a lady hanging out washing and a man hoeing in one of the small fields, spread as brown patches in a kind of green quilt, dark green where it appeared the fields may have been closed for hay, lighter green where the cows grazed. Looking down on this activity, with warm sunshine pouring on to them, it was very easy to imagine they were in a world of their own, the silence and lack of wind emphasised this, just a faint trace of distant birdsong was all that broke the stillness of their private world.

They sat down again, Jenny with her back resting against the rock, her breath now restored to normal, half closed her eyes and let the sun warm her. She sensed Rob leaning over her but she did not move, Rob now half turned towards her, gently placed his lips on hers, as he did so his arm went round her back and pulled her towards him, "Jenny darling, how long I have waited and dreamed of this day, how long is it since we really made love", "I guess almost two years, you know it is a long time since you could love me without a coughing fit", Jenny told him. As Rob again kissed her, Jenny felt his hand slowly lift her skirt and slide up her stocking , until she felt it warm and soft and so relaxed, on the bare skin above the stocking top.

Jenny felt relieved and so relaxed to think Rob was again interested in her as a lover, Jenny only then, realised how much she had missed their love life. Jenny still wore the loose pants that she had worn on the farm and as they continued to kiss she felt his hand continue to slide slowly up her leg, inside her pants and come to rest on her stomach, "Rob someone might come", Jenny protested,"Oh no my darling, no one ever has come here in all the weeks I have visited this place". Rob gently removed his hand, pulling Jenny to her feet he led her up three rock steps into a flat, grass covered place behind the rock, " no one will ever find us here", Rob told her, he took off his coat, placing it on the springy green floor for Jenny to sit on, sitting beside her they wrapped arms around one another and enjoyed the most passionate kiss Jenny could ever remember them sharing. Jenny allowed Rob to unbutton her blouse and unfasten her Bra. the next thing she knew was lying on Rob's coat, staring at a cloudless blue sky, with Rob leaning over her, holding a rapidly arousing breast, then bending further down, he again kissed her. Jenny could never remember if she ever thought about her plans to have another baby or not, but could remember arching her back whilst Rob slid off her panties, she could also remember thinking she had never seen Rob so aroused since goodness knows when. There was no fit of coughing to spoil their pleasure this time, just a wonderful warm feeling as Rob slid inside a more than willing Jenny, until with both of them worn and spent, they lay together looking at the sky.

Later they walked back down the hill to the hotel hand in hand, having arrived in their hotel room, it only took one more kiss to start them hurriedly undressing, to climb naked into the large comfortable double bed. The week passed, to Jenny, in a haze of blue skies, long walks, good food and good loving until a sad Rob kissed her on the morning of her departure. Rob was to start another course of medication, which Jenny suspected he had missed, during their week together, because the last night in the double bed, he had some difficulty making love to her. Before the Taxi came to take Jenny to the station, she had an appointment with Doctor Jurgen. Sitting in his office he asked Jenny if she had noticed any improvement in her husband, Jenny at once confirmed that she had, the Doctor told her he had expected her to say that, but warned her not to expect miracles.

The Doctor knew Rob was responding to his stay but it was mostly the lack of pressure and the good swiss air that was responsible. He went on to say that they had abandoned hope of retaining any use, however slight, from the first lung and that the second one was not responding to treatment as well as he hoped it would, indeed on some days he felt they were losing ground slightly. Tomorrow they were going to start a course of much more intensive treatment and he hoped that in a months time to be able to write and tell her an improvement had been noted. In the meantime if she wanted to visit again please consult him before coming, as she had done on this occasion, because Robs breaks in treatment were likely to be less frequent from now on. This conversation left Jenny just a little depressed but pleased that she had chosen this week to visit, now she just hoped that unknown to Rob, she could write, in a few weeks time, to tell him she was having a baby.

That was just what she was able to do, at the end of July Jenny felt confident enough to write a long loving letter to tell Rob he was going to be a father again. Jenny had already confided in Rob's parents and of course her own family, all of course offered help when she should feel the need of it. The rest of that year passed without incident, except that prices of the produce of Johnsons farm continued to fall and at the years end, Johnsons farm showed a loss on the year for the first time since well before the war. During early September Jenny had been to visit Rob again, but was shocked to find him so much worse than on her last visit. Doctor Jurgen told her he was undergoing some drastic treatment but the doctor was worried that Rob was not reacting favourably, however he hoped for an improvement in about six weeks, when the treatment was completed. Jenny came home, worried and realising that Rob must be much worse than she had realised. During the next few weeks Jenny worked to prepare the garage for the time she must be away to have her baby. The lady in the office was made more familiar with Jenny's bookkeeping system. Bertie was given more responsibility in ordering parts stock and new vehicles. Jenny's mother, Jane was asked and agreed to look over the accounts that Eve produced for the tea room and cafe, whilst Harry's petrol and oil accounts were taken directly to the office in Little Staunton.

Five weeks after Jenny's visit to Switzerland she received a letter from Doctor Jurgen who told her that Rob had completed his treatment, but was still very weak. There appeared to be no improvement from when Jenny was last there, but that was nor entirely unusual, many patients who were as ill as Rob, might expect to gain strength and live a reasonable life after a few weeks at home to gain strength. Finally the letter suggested that due to Rob's weak condition it would be advisable for someone to visit Switzerland and accompany him home. This last part of the letter worried Jenny, especially so since she was reminded most days now of how fit Rob had appeared during her visit of last May, even during her visit of six weeks ago he had not seemed too bad, just a little weaker she thought, but she could well remember how ill he had looked.

The following Sunday Jenny drove over to see Rob's parents, they were as concerned as Jenny was at the tone of Doctor Jurgens letter. They immediately asked Jenny if they could journey to Switzerland to accompany Rob home, believing Jenny should not make such a journey at this time, especially in view of the unknown condition of Rob. Jenny hesitated a little, but eventually common sense prevailed and she agreed to accept their offer. Jenny told Jane later, that she had realised it was unwise for her to undertake such a long journey in the final third of her pregnancy. Whilst she waited for her in laws to bring Rob home, Jenny concentrated on the garage and its accounts, finding that the profits were gradually improving, especially on the old army campsite, on the trunk road. Bertie suggested to her they should think about setting up the simple repair shop that Rob had originally planned. They were now getting four of five calls each week to breakdowns and Bertie thought more work would come if it was not so far to travel to Little Staunton. He also suggested the lorry that carried the tractors for demonstration and brought them in for repair, could be based there, whilst the mechanic who usually drove the lorry should be based there, where he could undertake many of the tractor repairs done in Little Staunton.

Jenny thought this one over for a night and then discussed it with Harry, he agreed with Bertie, being sure much more work would come once drivers realised there was a breakdown facility. That afternoon Jenny asked Bertie to give her an estimate of the cost of setting up such a facility. Before all these plans could be finished, an ashen faced and weak Rob arrived at Little Staunton station escorted by his parents. Hurrying him home, Jenny sat them down and put the kettle on, but before the tea was made, Rob was asleep. With the help of his parents, Jenny got him into bed, leaving him to sleep whilst Jenny was brought up to date on the journey, Doctor Jurgen had explained his weak condition was due to the treatment, this had been concentrated and heavy, but he now considered Rob recovered enough to travel but insisted he must not start work until much more of his strength had returned, if his cough returned later in the winter, a few more weeks at the clinic or its hotel might be most beneficial. Rob's mother, with tears in her eyes told Jenny she had never realised how ill Rob was and in spite of the doctors assurance, she really feared for his survival, she went on to say Rob had eaten very little on the journey and had slept most of the time. Robs parents agreed to stay the night, Jenny suggesting she would drive them home the next day.

After a good dinner, prepared jointly by Rob's mother and Jenny, they retired to bed, Rob was still asleep. The next morning Jenny woke early, washing and dressing she prepared some toast and coffee for Rob, taking it upstairs she shook him awake and sat with him whilst he tried to eat the toast, but only managed one piece, however he did manage to drink the coffee, Jenny put her arms round him and kissed him, but only got a weak response, soon after he fell asleep again. Jenny realising she could not leave him, telephoned Jane to see if she would drive Rob's parents home. Jenny sent for the doctor, who said just let him sleep and sure enough three days later Rob had recovered enough to come down stairs, Jenny was certainly relieved, even though her work at the garage was way behind.

Bertie had telephoned each morning to reassure her all was well and on the second day gave her a price for equipping the emergency workshop, Jenny told him to ahead and order the equipment. Rob gradually became stronger until one day he decided to ride with Jenny to the garage and then visit Harry and Eve at the trunk road depot. Rob was gradually getting better and both Jenny and his parents decided they should spend Christmas on the Graham farm. Jenny by this time was getting quite large and Rob decided he would drive them over to his parents on Christmas eve. This he did, apparently without effort, on Boxing day he had a bad day with his cough and an even worse night, eventually both Rob and Jenny left the bedroom to sit together in the warm kitchen, whilst Rob was treated with a bowl of Joe's inhaler. It was two days later before Rob was well enough to return to Little Staunton, by this time Jenny was extremely worried about Rob and the doctor did not give her much encouragement, telling Rob to stay in bed and rest, but saying to Jenny he was concerned that Rob's one lung had signs of inflamation in it.

It was now 1922, the new year brought news that John Deane and Jo, who had married in October were now expecting a baby, Janette and Rory, Johns parents were of course very pleased, Josie, Jo's mother whilst pleased, told Jo perhaps she should have waited a little longer. Jo smiled at her mother, gave her a kiss and reminded her that she seemed to remember her mother not worrying about having a baby a few years ago, yes, Josie told her, it was seven years ago and she did think circumstances were different. Josie now of course, had lost her daughters help with the poultry on Johnsons farm, but Tom had put one of the village ladies to help her each morning. Jo and John lived in the farmhouse on Spinney farm , just as Tom and Merri lived in Johnsons farm.

CHAPTER FOUR

Tragedy strikes and finances worsen

When the rabbit catching season finished in January, Walter and Elizabeth Knowles were married in Jensen church and had left for an unbelievable time of three weeks to visit Walters parents in Bavaria, to Elizabeth especially, it was the journey of a lifetime. To Walter it was even more special, not only had he a new wife, but he had not seen his parents for seven years, since the Kaiser had caused him to be enlisted into the Imperial German Army. Their journey to Bavaria took nearly four days, Elizabeth arrived almost exhausted but managed to show her happiness at meeting her new parents and was absolutely enchanted with their house, set in a clearing in the dark forest, it was a natural suntrap and its steep roof was something Elizabeth had never seen before. She was even more enchanted the next morning to awake and see a heavy covering of snow had arrived overnight, and to share a sleigh ride to the village shop for provisions with her new mother. Elizabeth had been trying so hard to learn the language of her new family and now she was getting her reward, although not fluent, she could speak sufficient of their language to enable conversation between Walters mother and herself during the christmas card like sleigh ride.

Rob was confined to bed for almost two weeks and then he did not leave the house until Jenny felt she must go to Johnsons farm for the birth of her baby, by this time Jenny felt her baby was overdue. But sure enough, nature looks after her own, her daughter Marjorie was born the beginning of the third week of February. Jane of course acting as midwife with Ma. assisting, as usual the doctor was invited to attend after the birth, he laughed at the two ladies who had delivered Marjorie, telling them he never knew why they needed him. "Well on this occasion we badly need you to look at Rob, he seems to me to be really ill", Jane told him. The doctor spent some time with Rob who was enthroned in one of the spare bedrooms, afterwards taking tea with them in the farm kitchen the doctor told them he was most concerned by Rob's health, he was reluctant to worry Jenny or indeed Rob himself, but he could only see one end and that was not too far away. Jane and Ma. were deeply upset, asking the doctor if there was indeed nothing that could be done, the doctor told them maybe Swiss air would be good for Rob, but he doubted if Rob was strong enough to make the journey. On leaving the doctor said he would look in over the next few days, ostensibly to see Jenny, but in reality to see Rob. Two days later Rob was having great difficulty in breathing and Jane felt she could delay no longer, telling Jenny Rob was really ill and that she was sending for the doctor. Jenny although still weak insisted on leaving her bed and going to sit with Rob. The doctor came and decided Rob must go to hospital, Jenny sat with him until the ambulance came, Jane went with Rob whilst Jenny telephoned his parents, who were shocked at the suddenness of Rob's collapse, although Jenny said she had known that Rob was really ill, but had not realised, with her own confinement imminent, just how ill poor Rob was.

The next day, with his parents at his bedside Rob gave up the struggle for life and Jenny, new mother that she was, also became a widow. It was a very difficult time on Johnsons farm, Jenny cried for hours, not just for Rob, but because she felt guilty that because of the birth of Marjorie she felt somehow she had neglected Rob. The decision of where to hold the funeral was difficult to make, but after her traumatic few hours Jenny felt better able to talk with Rob's parents. Jenny somehow sensed that they would like to have Rob's body interred with his ancestors in his local churchyard, when Jenny asked Rob's mother about this it immediately brought tears to her eyes as she gripped Jenny's hand. Later Jenny explained that Rob had hardly had time to settle in Little Staunton and if David should take up the Graham farm, as they all wished, then it would be wrong for one member of the family to be buried in another and distant place. With the garage closed for the day, Robs funeral took place at the end of February, Jenny, supported by her family and, of course, Rob's family also, put on a brave face but upon returning home she realised how much she had lost and how little she had left from the brief years they had spent together, just memories and two lovely children, one of whom may leave her in the years to come, for a life on the Graham farm.

Walter had discussed the possibility of staying in Germany with both Elizabeth and his parents, Elizabeth had not objected to the idea, although it was probable her experiences of just a week or so of living there, were still clouded by euphoria of living in a new and lovely place. But Walters father had painted a completely different picture, to that they had seen locally, he told them Germany was going through a very bad time, food expensive, heavy unemployment in the towns and every week it seemed the weekly wages bought less and less, he strongly advised them to stay in England. But if things did get better his letters to them would reflect that and maybe at that time they may consider it again. Soon after their return Elizabeth told both Walter and her mother she was almost certainly having a baby, Jessie looked at her asking "so soon", Elizabeth told her she had taken no precautions during her visit to Germany, believing Walters first child should be conceived there. If she had found on her return, that a baby was not on the way then they would probably waited a while.

Jenny after a few unhappy and lethargic weeks following Rob's death, had managed to pull herself together and was now an active mum and garage owner. The garage was becoming a successful business and Jenny was very proud of her achievement, the original representative from Ford had now retired and a new man now called on the garage, mostly Bertie dealt with him, only on rare occasions did Jenny see him. Ma. now well over seventy years old still looked after the accounts, but had told Jane that she felt unable to carry on as she had done up to now. Ma. thought they should have a full time lady to work in the kitchen, so Jane could take over the accounts completely.

One day in May 1922 Merri did not return on time from the morning milk run, it was a very wet day and both Tom and Joe were working on the mowing machines in the shed, preparing them for the hay harvest. By this time Merri was almost an hour late and as it had eased off raining a little, Tom decided he would take the bicycle and go to look if he could see her. As he turned out of the farm gate the rain started to come down even heavier than before, however Tom decided he was already wet and might as well carry on, after about a mile towards Little Staunton he saw the lorry standing on the side of the road. Arriving with it he found Merri struggling to undo a wheel nut on the left hand rear wheel, Merri looked up saying "am I glad to see you I just cannot undo these damn nuts", she told him what a job she had to jack up the vehicle having found, to her dismay, that the rear wheel had gone flat. She had stopped the lorry at the side of the road and had to lie down to reach the axle under which she knew the jack must be placed, the side of the road was of course running in water so she had her clothes soaked just lying there, but worse still, the water she was lying in had drained from the road surface and smelled strongly of horses urine, so poor Merri now was not only soaked through but smelled strongly of horses also. Tom soon had the offending wheel nuts undone and the spare wheel fitted, by this time of course they were both so wet that water just ran down their trouser legs and into their boots. The bicycle was thrown into the back of the truck along with the damaged wheel and they set off for home, soon arriving in the horse yard.

Joe volunteered to take the second delivery and also get the wheel mended, Merri telling him she was wet through and frozen, Tom and Merri walked into the kitchen, but found it empty, Tom love, Merri said will you run me a bath, I smell like a stable, Tom went upstairs to run a bath and take off his own soaked clothes whilst Merri took off her wet and smelly overalls, leaving them in the kitchen. Entering the bedroom Merri took off the rest of her soaked clothing and walked into the bathroom, Tom was running the bath and whilst it filled he turned to her, taking her in his arms he kissed her, saying " you really have had a bad morning dear", Merri replied yes but it is better now at least I have got you to keep me company. Merri lay luxuriating in the hot water whilst Tom bent over her kissing and stroking her, as she warmed up he could feel her passions rising, the nipples on her breasts becoming hard and her lips more demanding, see if you can get in the bath with me she told him. With some care and a few giggles from Merri Tom managed to lie with her and enjoy the lovely warm water, "what a good job your dad suggested having a bathroom to each bedroom when the house was modernised" Merri said. After a while they both climbed out of the bath and dried themselves, "come on Tom let us just lie on the bed for a few minutes, I just must have another kiss". As they lay together Tom realised Merri was really aroused as indeed he was, kissing was no longer enough and as Merri wriggled in anticipation Tom reached over her and soon entered her, finding the desired warm and loving place he knew was available. Later they dressed and Merri made tea in the kitchen, afterwards returning to work, but that night in bed Merri told him she thought they had made a mistake, they should have used a protector that morning. But she had not thought at the time, "well I did think you were particularly affectionate", Tom told her but are you really sure "Oh yes but maybe it will not work again, after all I got away with it last time". By the end of June Merri knew that she "had not got away with it", and she told Jane all about her problems with the puncture and its consequences. Jane just laughed and told her not to worry, it would be lovely to have another Grandchild, perhaps Merri might think of doing it again next year, "Oh no not if I can help it, but then I suppose I could not help it this year".

The harvest went well, Merri not being too far advanced in her pregnancy, drove one of the cutting tractors, but still it was a long harvest but thankfully the weather was good, although the profit was still depressed and Joe thought they would do well to break even this year. Merri had her third child in February, Theresa May Johnson, all had gone well and Merri was soon up and about again, Tom enjoying again the midnight feeds and a cuddle from Merri before they went off to sleep again. Merri was being very careful though and soon put a stop to Tom's loving ways, insisting he used a protector and take no chances.

Just as Ma. had suggested, they found that one of the farm women who lived with her brother and his wife would be willing to come and live in the farmhouse, both to work in the kitchen and look after the children, so Jane could concentrate on the accounts, Jane Knowles had by now given up the job and only took casual work on the farm in busy times. The next few years passed with considerable worry, crops seemed to be worth less money each year, but the farm managed to make a small profit most years, until 1928 when the profit showed increased volume.

Late in that year the Ford representative asked for an appointment with Jenny, arriving in mid morning Jenny took him to her office where "John Patterson" for that was his name, gave her an invitation to visit Cambridge to inspect the new Ford model A car and its equivalent lorry version. He also hoped that the new tractor, to be made at Cork in Irish Free State, would also be on view, Jenny told him she would certainly be there and bring Mr. Johnson with her who represented the major shareholder in the garage. The garage had very few new vehicles for almost a year now, the tractor had not been made in any quantity since 1926 and the Model T car had ceased production a long time ago, but now a new car and tractor probably meant more work at the garage. The trunk road depot. was now proving successful, Harry was the acknowledged manager and Eve had the lorry cafe and the ladies and gentlemans tea rooms running like clockwork.

On their return from Cambridge both Jenny and Joe were excited about the new vehicles, no specific orders had been sought or placed, but Ford informed all the dealers it would not be very long before the vehicles were in free supply and each dealer would soon be informed of their first deliveries. Johnsons farm still had its evening meetings and one was scheduled for the day after Jenny and Joe had been to visit Cambridge, Jenny came but the children stayed at home in the care of a lady who had lost her husband in the war and never remarried, she now acted as housekeeper and childrens nurse for Jenny. After describing the vehicles Joe suggested it was now a good time to change the garage around, Jenny had told him she had two thousand pounds in the bank, in addition to the money in a current account for day to day running of the business. It was Joe's idea that the garage in Little Staunton should concentrate on cars only, and the trunk road depot. should handle lorries and tractors. Joe thought that a bank loan of one thousand pounds along with the two thousand in the bank would be ample to build a new workshop and also a new house for Harry and Eve, leaving their present living quarters and the current workshop as storage and a small showroom.

Tom and Merri wanted to know more about the new tractors, as Tom pointed out the current two Fordson tractors were about eight years old and had done a great deal of work. Joe explained that the new model had four important new features, magneto ignition, no trembler coils now, an engine governor, a water pump and as they could see from the literature, mud wings covering the whole of the rear wheels, with tool boxes built into them. With still three thousand pounds in investments it was decided Johnsons farm should buy two of the new tractors and that Jenny and Joe should visit the bank manager to arrange a loan for the garage.

Gil and Merri were by this time successfully regulating their love life quite well, Gil had seen an advertisement in a ladies magazine, suggesting it was now possible to control the size of your family, she had written for details. In reply had come information on a new light latex rubber sheath and a free sample, along with the address of a chemist in Staunton who stocked "this ultra modern method of birth control". Gil and Merri had enthusiastically adopted this new product and up to this time the results had been very successful. Elizabeth Knowles, or rather Lieber as her name now was, also had converted to their use after the birth of her son James Otto. John Deane and Jo had no need to use this new aid, Jo had a difficult birth, her daughter Joan, now usually called Joanne had meant that in spite of the doctor and then the hospitals best efforts it seemed unlikely she would ever be able to increase the size of her family.

Jenny and Joe had no difficulty in borrowing the thousand pounds required, indeed the bank manager had offered more if it were needed. So in early 1929 the garage development was completed and Johnsons farm had two new tractors, the old ones now joined the old Mogul in retirement, the other Mogul of course was still being used to drive the threshing set. Frank Simpson had been trying to persuade them to buy one of the new International 10/20 tractors to replace the Mogul. Partly due to caution in spending money and partly because the 10/20 had steel wheels with deep lugs on the wheels, thus not being able to run on public roads, they had resisted this temptation and stayed with the Mogul. By the time all these purchases and changes had taken place, the newspapers were telling of a financial crash on the New York stock exchange. That night Tom brought up the problems in New York, asking Joe if he thought it would affect England and the farming industry, Joe, for once had no definite answer. He thought it may mean more wheat at even lower cost would arrive in England, but thought the factories may be worse hit due to much cheaper American goods arriving in England. Although he supposed that may increase unemployment which would mean less money to spend by the working population, which in turn may mean less or cheaper food would be bought. Merri and Jane listening to this conversation criticised the politicians for allowing all these things to happen, especially the suicides of business men being reported from America.

On the strength of this conversation they decided the two final wheat stacks should be threshed as soon as possible and the corn sold. Elizabeth still fed the drum but Jill no longer worked with her, Jill's place had been taken by Merri, whilst on threshing days it was Tom who took over Merri's lorry job. With the wheat ready to sell, it was found that the price had fallen dramatically, but even so they decided to sell it, but at surely what was a loss. By mid 1931 both Rory Deane and the estate farm were losing money in quite large amounts, because of its greater variety of crops Johnsons farm was not losing so much. Rorys cure was to sack all the workers except the cowman and leave the farm to stagnate, the estate rearrange its work force, between the game keeping side and estate management and service departments and the farm, the result of this was that six men retired and all overtime was cut out, so the estate could survive reasonably well. The fact that by Rory leaving much of the farm to become unproductive, the amount of milk he sold to Johnsons farm fell quite considerably, this helped Johnsons farm, Rory had been selling 100 gallons each day to the farm but now he was supplying only twenty. The London dairy had, for the first time ever, reduced their demand to the minimum they were contracted to buy, eighty gallons and even that at a lower price. Johnsons farm dairy was also down in its demands by about forty per cent, as hard times began to hit the customers.

Johnsons farm now had a surplus of unsold milk, this was fed to the pigs which initially increased the supply of pig produce, which were unsaleable so the pig population was reduced by half. A quarter of the milking herd were sent to market, but each beast made only a few pounds, the market being overloaded with them from almost every farm in the district. At the begining of the harvest crops looked good but Joe and Tom wondered what they could do with the crops now almost ready to gather. By the end of the year Johnsons farm accounts showed a loss of over one thousand pounds, leaving only the same amount in the bank as a cushion against bankruptcy. Johnsons farm had over twenty workers, non of which had been sacked, both Jane and Tom now told Joe it was time to consider this. During early January 1932 the usual dinner and harvest festival was organised, but this year only a sandwich and home made pie buffet was to be provided along with the usual barrel of beer and tea. Ma. was not present, the first dinner she had missed, Ma. was confined to bed, old age and weariness she told them. When everyone was assembled Joe stood in front of the company and asked them to consider what he was going to say very carefully. Joe started off by reminding them that no one on Johnsons farm had, as yet, lost their job, but this situation could not continue. The weekly wage bills were much too high, the farm had done all it could to reduce costs, no new machinery was to be bought, no cattle food, no new stock not even poultry, no fencing materials or gates, in fact he anticipated the farm would spend no money during 1932, other than fuel for the vehicles and as little of that as possible.

Now Joe wanted them to listen very carefully because he felt the wage bill must be halved, of course if anyone had another job to go to, then please give notice and leave. He, Joe, had a proposal to make to them, he did not want any of them to leave or be sacked. Joe therefore proposed that wages be cut by half, to compensate for this he suggested each family should take from the farm milk, bacon, ham, pork, eggs, chicken meat and when available a joint of beef, in addition the mill would grind wheat as fine as possible to provide flour, wholewheat, of course and each family could have whatever potatoes they needed whilst they were available. The risk to Johnsons farm was that each worker might not "put his back" into working under these circumstances as they had before, but Joe felt certain they would act with honesty, some might feel inclined to sell or give away food to their relatives, Joe had to say if that happened instant dismissal would automatically follow, with a requirement that any property belonging to the farm must be vacated at once. Finally Joe told them that if any worker felt unable to accept these terms then they were able to give notice and leave. He then thanked them for their efforts over the past year and hoped this coming year would bring better conditions and the restrictions he had just announced would soon be over.

Joe, Tom ,Merri and Jane sat together at one table, hoping to give all the staff a chance to talk over what he had just announced, later they began to circulate as they usually did at this annual function, several families quickly agreed to Joe's proposal and by the next midday everyone had agreed. Walter came to Joe the next day asking if he should return to Germany with his wife Elizabeth, Joe told him he should stop in England and on Johnsons farm, the conditions in Germany were, most probably even worse than those here.

At the end of 1932 Jane could only report a loss of nearly five hundred pounds, the biggest cause of this was the rent paid for Riverside and Moorside farms but both Tom and Joe were very reluctant to give either farm up. Although it was possible, as Joe recognised, that if they suggested it to Lord Jensen he might give them a years grace on the rent, not being able to let them again under these financial conditions, but Joe was reluctant to add to the problems the estate must already be suffering from. During the early spring of 1933 they had to send for the doctor to Ma. who by now had lapsed into the habit of only coming downstairs in the afternoons, but now they found, one morning she was hardly lucid.

The doctor told them he could find no evidence of any problem, it was his opinion Ma. was just worn out and if they left her to rest she may well recover in a day or two, he could make arrangements for her to be transported to hospital if they wished, as one, both Jane and Joe told him not even to think about it. Ma. did in fact recover but came down to sit in the kitchen less and less, until one morning Jane took her morning tea, but found her mother unconscious. Both Jane and Joe sat with her all day, whilst other members of the family came and went, Ma. never opened her eyes again, but they both held her hand and occasionally spoke to her and at one time she turned her head towards them, giving comfort to them that their words may be heard, even if the response was so weak.

Joe and Jane stayed with her, but at eight o'clock that night Ma. gave up life on earth and so, with all the family at Johnsons farm, her long and wonderfully generous life came to an end. Joe was even more devastated than anyone, both he and Ma. had adopted one another as mother and son, there was a deep understanding between them and Joe was now feeling the loss very keenly indeed. The funeral was held five days later, the farm men led by Joe and Tom carried the coffin to Jensen church where later Ma. was laid to rest with her husband Tom, killed on the farm they both loved, thirty or so years before. Many were the mourners, the church was full so was the farmhouse, after the funeral and the many mourners had left, Jane, Joe, Tom and Merri sat in the office, but had not the heart to talk of the farm or the future.

After a short time Tom said he was going for a walk, Merri left her chair to walk with him, Jane and Joe just sat in glum silence, the farm workers had not been asked to return to work in the afternoon, just the seymour family who milked the dairy herd. Tom and Merri walked over the home field and along the cart track leading to Moorside farm, it was a late April sunny afternoon so Tom turned off the track

114

behind the spinney and eventually on to Riverside farm land, as they walked, hand in hand in silence, they suddenly became aware of large rain spots falling, quickly becoming an April downpour. Quick Tom told Merri, run for the old shed, dashing inside they were out of the rain and soon found themselves sitting on a pile of straw waiting for the shower to pass. Maybe it was the trauma of the funeral, or just that Merri realised suddenly she would never see Ma. again, but Tom realised Merri was in tears, Tom had never seen her cry before, he was taken totally unawares. Quickly putting his arm around her he took an handkerchief from his pocket to dry her tears, then gently kissed her, he could still feel the tears again running down her cheeks but with her arms around him he could not easily pull away to wipe her tears away again. As they quietly kissed he could feel Merri become more aroused and with lips constantly joining and withdrawing, he found he badly wanted to make love to her. Eventually Merri lay back on the straw, undid the buttons on her blouse and exposed her breasts, Tom kissed them alternating with her lips, Merri soon whispered "love me Tom", as he kissed her. Tom undid his trousers and as Merri eased herself up he slid her panties down and Merri put her arms round him. Her skirt round her waist and Toms trousers lying on the straw they abandoned themselves to love. An hour passed, the sun now shining again outside and a happy and satisfied couple kissing inside they began to unwind, putting on their clothes and brushing off bits of straw, Merri said "Tom I feel so much better now".

Two days later they all visited the solicitor, Mathew Wright having now retired, the man who would officiate was his son James Wright. With the usual solicitors language he offered his condolences to the family, he then remarked that Ma. had put an unusual request in her will, she had left no money or shares to Mr. Joseph Johnson, at his own request. But she had charged that those who inherited the farm must be sure Mr. Johnson would never be turned away and that he should have a home in Johnsons farm whilst ever it was in the family, for the rest of his life. The same conditions did also apply to her daughter Jane, although of course she had a ten per cent share in the farm. The farm itself was to be left to Thomas Johnson with the exception that his wife Meredith should own ten per cent in her own name. The shares owned by Johnsons farm in Little Staunton Motors should be disposed of as follows, ten per cent to Mrs. Gil Simpson, ten per cent to Mrs. Jennifer Graham and the remaining seventeen per cent to Mr. Thomas Johnson. Mr. Wright told them he had already arranged the share transfers and all he needed were their signatures.

They returned to the farm and after tea met in the office, Gil and Jenny had not expected to be left a larger share in the garage but were of course pleased, Jenny realising that now she was the largest share holder. Tom was amazed to have the farm left in his name, he had not expected to inherit until Joe died, always he had thought Joe had the controlling interest, Merri was also very surprised by having a share left in her name, but Jane explained that the wife of the Johnson currently owning the farm always had a ten per cent share. Jane had that percentage inherited from her father and would leave it to Tom in her will. Tom turning to his father asked why he had no share in Johnsons farm, Joe assured him that Johnsons farm was his life, he had married the only part of the farm that he would ever need.

Merri looking at Joe, said she realised that the success of the farm rested on Joes shoulders and she hoped the farm would run just as it always had done, dear Ma., did not need to make Joe a permanent home in her will, he would always have a home with Merri.

After this upset Johnsons farm went on much as usual, but Joe made sure most of the daily decisions were made by Tom, only making suggestions on rare occasions. During the autumn England started to recover, it was wheat and imported grain that gave hope to the farming community. America was still in depression and the climate had not helped, much of the grain harvest had been reduced by the tremendous dust storms sweeping the grain belt, also many farmers had either gone bankrupt or just given up farming, the price of crops being so low. These problems helped the price of wheat to rise to an economic level and with just a little confidence returning to the factory owners Joe noticed a slow rise in the demand for other farm products.

Johnsons farm had always kept the calves born to the dairy herd, although between nine and eighteen months old, they had been killed to provide, not only the staff with meat but also some were sold to the butcher. Tom now suggested to his dad one day, he was thinking of keeping about forty of the heifers now about one year old, to increase the dairy herd, believing milk was again going to be in demand, especially with talk of the new milk marketing scheme to be introduced in the future. At the end of 1933 with the farm just making a small profit again, Tom, now recognised by all as the farmer, made the speech at Johnsons farm annual dinner.

He told the staff, full wages would be paid again, strangely enough it was not universally welcomed, at least two families told Joe later that they would miss the good food that they did not have to purchase. During the two years of half pay there had been minimal overtime worked, this had left the farm with an untidy appearance, some overgrown hedges and a few defective drains. The state Johnsons farm found itself in was nothing to the state of the Deane's Spinney farm. Half of the fields had not been used and were overgrown with coarse grasses and weeds, whilst most of the hedges were towering high and, in some cases twelve feet wide. Having had no staff for two years, Rory and son John with the help of John's two sisters, although working hard, stood no chance of keeping the farm in any kind of state that might allow it to make a quick recovery. To make matters worse, at least as far as workers were concerned, the two girls were both engaged to be married to farmers sons, one of them in the spring of 1934, the other during the summer.

Joe did not criticise Rory for getting the farm in such a state, he realised that he had no knowledge of the Deane's financial position at the time they had sacked all the workers, but Joe did think, privately, that Rory had gone rather too far. The crisis on Spinney farm came quite suddenly in February, John and Rory had set themselves to recover about fifty acres of the neglected land, and during the winter had managed to plough it. They then started to side the hedges, leaving them high and planning to cut and lay them in the autumn, there were a great deal of cut thorns to be burnt during that February, the plan was to complete this job in time to plant oats and barley on the fifty acres. Whilst John was preparing the land that had been in production throughout, Rory was burning the thorns. It was a damp and miserable February and Rory had a very bad cold, but refusing to give up, had continued with the bonfires. Maybe it was the smoke or just that he neglected the cold, but one afternoon he returned to the farm, weak and shivering telling his wife, Janette, he could not carry on, she got him to bed with a hot drink but he could not get warm and was having difficulty breathing. The doctor came and told Janette Rory had pneumonia, leaving some medicine the doctor said he would visit the next morning. This he did and immediately telephoned for an ambulance telling Janette if he was to have any chance of recovery then the hospital was the only hope. It proved a vain hope, Rory died two days later, the family were, of course devastated, indeed not just the family but the whole village, not the least the Johnsons. Tom was soon over to see his friend John and to offer any assistance he could, Janette of course made tea and as they sat together with Jo, Johns wife, John suggested that he may have to ask Johnsons farm to take over some of the land. Tom said he would think about it and Janette said they did not yet know how Rory's will might read.

That spring Johnsons farm had contracted to grow twenty acres of sugar beet, a new crop to them, but based on a new sugar factory being built about five miles away. It promised to be a profitable venture, they had the option to buy back some of the processed beet pulp for cattle food and the green tops cut off the bottoms could also be used to feed the dairy herd. The crop represented a heavy labour content but to help cover this, Johnsons farm had decided not to grow turnips this year. Tom was now the mainstay of the farm, Joe was 64 years old and Jane 58, whilst both Tom and Merri were 34, of their children Jay was 15 and Will 14, both were involved in the farm. They usually attended the evening office meetings, just as Jenny, Gil and Tom had when they were young. Jay and Will now were regularly driving the tractors, especially in the harvest, leaving Billy to build the stacks and Harry to pick and help load the harvest waggons in the fields. Jay would often help in the house, whilst Will now finished with school was always busy, usually with Joe, on the farm. Tessa May, known to them all as Tess was devoted to Jane and usually found around her. Of the other workers on Johnsons farm, Walter Seymour the cowman was 65, but Joe's idea put in practice before the war that the Seymour family should run the dairy herd, was now paying off. Walter two sons and daughter Janice were involved, Walter would retire soon leaving the two sons now in their early thirties to take over. Janice was engaged to be married and so would leave in the summer. Fred the elder of the two sons lived in a farm cottage vacated by Bill and Jill Worsley, whilst Adrian had rented a cottage from the estate.

The reading of Rory's will left the farm to John and two hundred pounds each to the daughters, the solicitor told them Rory had stated that the farm must go to John and the girls being married to Farmers sons would be well provided for, but Rory had felt he must leave them a token payment. Obviously, the solicitor told them, Rory had not known he would have passed on before the girls were married. This raised the question if either of them wished to challenge the will, but from what the solicitor told them, that would be a most unwise course of action. The farm was in a run down condition and probably not saleable at any realistic price, they would probably be better served to accept the will as it was, or legal fees may take up any money realised. John and Jo, concerned about their sisters well being, though they may be, had to point out that it would almost bankrupt the farm to find the four hundred pounds to pay the sisters. The situation was left for them to discuss at home, both sisters were concerned about John and Jo's future as they were about their mother Janette and what would happen to her, they all left it to John to find a solution to the problem. Poor John, it was a problem he had not expected and to make matters worse, he had no son to follow him and probably would never have one now, to give him the incentive to carry on the farm. All he could hope for was that daughter Joanne might marry a farmers son and carry on the farm, even though under another name.

The result of the family discussion was that John should see if Ton Johnson would take 250 acres rent free for three years and hold it as security for guaranteeing a loan of four hundred pounds from the bank to pay off the two sisters. This would leave John with 350 acres and six hundred and fifty pounds to farm it with. Discussing this one evening with Tom, it was agreed they would jointly visit the bank manager to set up the deal and that Johnsons farm would then immediately take over the 250 acres. It was now left to Tom to decide what to do with the land, untouched for so long, this included 100 acres of grassland only rough grazed. Tom decided Billy and Harry should plough the grassland immediately, whilst Will and Jay used the Two old Fordson tractors to finish working for the spring crops, most of which were already set, on Johnsons farm. He then consulted Joe who agreed with Tom, that the other 150 acres should be ploughed and summer fallowed, then drilled with winter wheat in the autumn, both men believing that John Deane would never take back the 250 acres. During the 1930's with agriculture in dire problems the government decided it must intervene at least with some help for the dairy industry and so the milk marketing board came into being. This acted as a buying agency, guaranteeing a basic price for the amount of milk each farm was contracted to supply, paying more in the winter, when milk was more expensive to produce and less in the summer, when it was cheaper to produce. It then sold the milk to the dairies at a controlled price, thus the housewife was protected from wildly varying prices. This new arrangement made very little difference to Johnsons farm, but was a great advantage to John Deane who could increase his milk yield considerably, now having the confidence that a guaranteed market and price would offer.

CHAPTER FIVE

War looms near

In 1936 both Tom and Joe knew another war was possible, the civil war in Spain was filling the newspapers with horror stories and pictures, plus the stories of Herr. Hitlers growing power in Germany. In 1938 after a few steady years of profit, Tom decided they must modernise the arable equipment, in 1933 a new Fordson tractor was introduced, in 1937 an improved model with rubber tyres came out. Tom decided they must buy two of these new orange tractors, he spoke to Jenny and a price was agreed, the two model F Fordsons went in exchange and the two Irish ones took up the space by the unused Mogul.

One evening Tom raised the question of money during the office meeting, telling them he felt they should buy a new threshing machine with one of the new balers to deal with the straw and a new more powerful tractor to drive it. Tom pointed out war, in his opinion, was almost inevitable and Joe agreed with him, but the cost would be almost two thousand pounds, Jane reminded them that there was still one thousand pounds invested, that had been there since the first world war and in addition, they had almost two thousand pounds in the current account.

Jane thought this was not overmuch money to think about spending so much on equipment, but could see the advantage of modernising, because if a war came prices could well escalate and machinery become very scarce. The wheat price was still reasonable, so Joe thought they should order the equipment for delivery in August and then thresh a considerable amount of wheat to help pay the bill, that was the plan adopted. An International W30 tractor was ordered from Frank Simpson at a price agreed so Simpson Machinery would take back the Mogul still being used to drive the old set. A new threshing drum and baler plus two new ploughs were ordered from Jenny who had now a Ransomes franchise to back up the Fordson one.

About this time Tom called on John Deane to enquire what was to be done about the 250 acres Johnsons farm had been using rent free. John declared he was just beginning to become solvent again and had almost finished paying off the bank loan, they were at last, living a comfortable life and he did not want to take on the other 250 acres. Would Johnsons farm pay the same rent for it as they paid the Jensen estates for Riverside and Moorside farms. Tom said he thought they would but the rental period must start from the January the first 1939, this John agreed with as did Jo and Janette. "By the way, we are seeing quite a bit of Will these days" Jo told Tom, asking if he knew, "no do you object", Tom asked "Oh no, we love him like a son he is always welcome, we think Joanne is quite smitten with him", Tom suggested they were quite a good match, but perhaps a trifle young.

January 1939 came and an agreement with John Deane for the rent of the 250 acres was signed, thus Johnsons farm now totalled 1200 acres. Joe sat at the desk he had so painstakingly made many years ago, his thoughts turning back to the 1890's when Johnsons farm had extended to only 450 acres, he thought of the good times he had shared with Ma. and his wife Jane, the children they had produced, the grandchildren, they had provided. Joe thought how lucky he had been that day in Little Staunton market, as he stood with a corn dolly pinned to his jacket, denoting he was available for work. How Tom Johnson had approached him and Joe had entered Johnsons farm kitchen for the first time. How he had been introduced to a young Ma. and Jane as little more than a school girl, only then had he found out that he was to work on a farm bearing his name. Joe let his thoughts wander back over the years and marvelled at how lucky he had been. How Tom Johnson had been killed falling from a hay cart and how Joe had eventually married Jane and become more and more involved with the farm. He had bought the first lorry, the first tractor, how he had , right out of the blue, put in a bid for the garage and how they had made it grow since then. How the village of Jensen had developed, some new cottages, the new main sewer and mains water enabling them to have flush toilets for the first time, how electricity had finally reached them, so many memories, such an interesting and rewarding life.

These thoughts were interrupted by Jane coming into the office, telling Joe she wanted to talk to him, Jane produced a leaflet of a motor cycle, a 250cc BSA. Jane suggested they should buy it for Will, Jane knew he had been keen on it for some time, but that he did not have the thirty pounds needed to buy it. Yes Joe told her, it was a good idea, but surely they should also do something for Jay as well. It so happened that Joe had seen, in the garage an Austin seven car, Jenny had priced it at forty pounds, it had been taken in against a new Ford eight. Jay had passed her driving test the last summer, so Joe thought they could afford to buy both vehicles from their private money, but he told Jane they should talk to Tom and Merri first.

Having spoken to Tom and Merri about these vehicles, and

having no objection raised, a few days later, Jane drove Will into Little Staunton where he was flabbergasted to find he was the owner of a new motor cycle, before he left for home Jane bought him a heavy coat and a pair of gauntlet gloves, so after some instruction from the shop man, Will left for home. Unknown to Will, Joe had asked Jay to go with him to the garage, where to her amazement she was presented with the key and documents for the Austin seven, beautifully cleaned by Pip's assistant. Although Pip still cleaned new vehicles she could not always cope with the volume, so she now had a local girl to help her. Of course Pip and Jenny were old friends dating back to before Jenny became involved with the garage.

Jay left for home and Joe went to visit Frank Simpson to collect some spare parts, Jane arrived soon after, Jenny asked her to come into the office. Sitting together with a coffee, Jenny told Jane that John Patterson, the Ford representative had taken her out for dinner on a few occasions, but that she was not in a serious relationship with him, but felt that John might be getting serious. Jenny was telling Jane this because she did not want Jane to hear that her daughter was going out with a man, Jane laughing, suggested surely Jenny deserved some male company, after being a widow for nearly seventeen years. Asking after her Grandchildren, Jenny told Jane that David was just finishing two years at an agricultural college and then would go to live with the Graham family and eventually take over the farm, Andrew, Rob's brother, had never married and was still devoted to the dairy herd. Marjorie (Margy) was starting to work at the garage when her schooling was finished at Easter. Returning home Jane drove the Ford V8 car, bought a year ago, into the open shed where it was

126

kept, to find an Austin seven and a new motor cycle being inspected by the family, both Grandchildren rushed up to Jane with a kiss and voluble thanks for their gifts.

Sugar beet was now a valuable crop to Johnsons farm and this year they had contracted to grow forty acres, with thirty acres of mangolds and thirty acres of potatoes, Johnsons farm was likely to be under some pressure to hoe and harvest these crops. Luckily there were now some Irish labouring gangs doing the rounds and both Tom and Joe hoped one of these would be available at the right time. It was not usually too difficult, because Johnsons farm, as they had always done, provided a midday meal for the hoeing gang and for the last two years the same gang had come to do the hoeing and last year they had come to help with the harvesting and had promised to come agin this year.

During the summer it became more and more obvious that a war with Germany must surely come, Johnsons farm had never, since the bad years of 1930 to 1932 bought very much artificial manure, but this year Tom had decided to increase its use, believing a war, if it came would surely increase the price of crops. This year, 1939, they had not to thresh the wheat early, to pay for machinery, as they had in 1938, Tom believed if a record crop could be harvested much of the wheat could remain in the stack until spring. It was at this time that the government decided to start and prepare agriculture for war, each county had an agricultural committee and so they were extended and strengthened. An arrangement was made to alter their title to "War Agricultural Committee", if war broke out , and sweeping powers were prepared to come into force at that time.

The corn harvest was good and by the end of August most

of Johnsons farm corn was cut, then came Neville Chamberlains historic broadcast, telling an anxious nation that we were at war with Germany. The immediate reaction was to look for air raids, the harvest workers carried their gas masks, hung on the harvest waggons, gas masks were hung in the cowsheds at milking time and left in handy places in the houses at night. The first event of importance to the farm was the notification that the War Ag., as it had become known, would allocate a threshing round to the Johnsons farm set, to be sure maximum use was being made of this scarce resource. Then they were made aware that one of the County field officers would be calling to advise them on the crops they were to produce, this caused an explosion from Tom, but Joe calmed him down, telling him it was only an extension of what he had done in the first world war. But in the main this was forgotten as the farm concentrated on finishing the harvest, except that Tom was daily expecting a letter telling him of what the threshing set had been allocated to do. One wet day Tom took the car and visited ten neighbours, including John Deane and Jensen estate, the result was that the threshing set had almost a complete winters work planned. The next day Tom wrote to the War Ag., telling them of the commitments and asking what more they could do.

That evening in the office the discussion centred around how to staff the threshing set, in view of the full winters work planned. The new drum had a self feeding attachment so only one person was required on top. The second person being used to place the needles between the bales and thread the wires that fastened the compressed straw into the solid bales the machine produced. Tom decided that Billy should take over the threshing set full time, when he had built the corn stacks, although he was now sixty five years old, but still fit and able. Tom also decided to see if his son Jacky would also work on the set, perhaps to take over if Billy felt, at some future date, he could not continue. Harry Downs the other tractor driver now also over sixty was to be asked to look after the hedges and drains. Will and Jay were to take over the two Fordson tractors and become the mainstay of the cultivation team. It was late September that John Patterson called on the garage to inform Jenny vehicles for the home market were about to become very scarce, he could predict a few Anglia cars, three of four lorries and six tractors, after that he believed vehicles for the home market would only be available against government permits. He also asked Jenny if he could pick her up at seven pm. and take her to dinner, although Jenny had been out with him many times over the last eighteen months, she could sense something different about this invitation. Sure enough John arrived promptly at seven, Jenny invited him in and offered a sherry, John accepted and they sat making small talk until obviously, if they were to make the table reservation they must leave.

On the journey to the rather swish restaurant about eight miles away, Jenny told him she had decided she must order the vehicles he had suggested may be available. After a very good meal they sat repleat and comfortable with coffee on the table, John reached over to hold Jenny's hand, asking if she might consider becoming engaged to him and, of course, eventually to marry him. Jenny had somehow known something along these lines may come up to-night, she asked him for a few days to think about it, believing she must tell Margy before accepting. As John left Jenny at her door, he took both her hands in his, telling her he would be visiting the next Monday. Jenny disengaged her hands and kissed him.

Will and Jay had, of course been using their new vehicles to some effect, Will to visit the Deane farm and persuade Joanne to ride on the pillion with him, whilst Jay had been to the shops, visiting friends and to dance's in Little Staunton. Both Will and Jay were excited at the prospect of becoming the main tractor drivers and as soon as the first field of corn was cleared they started their new careers. One October day the Jensen Estate manager, James Thurlow, arrived at Johnsons farm to inform Tom that the R.A.F., were planning to build an airfield on the old army camp, on the opposite side of the road to the garage, but had not shown any interest in the land that Johnsons farm rented alongside the garage. The garage was now a large and flourishing business, not only the petrol and cafe operation, but the repair shop, whilst the truck and tractor operations were growing strongly. So much so that Jenny had organised a lady to look after the book keeping on a full time basis, whilst Harry operated solely as manager.

A couple of days after Tom had been told about the projected airfield, he was in Little Staunton and decided he should tell Jenny about this new development. Jenny then told him of the new vehicles, which may be the last ones in free supply, Tom at once said he felt they should buy two of the lorries. He had also seen a new cultivator standing with other machinery and felt they should also buy that. Returning home he sent Jay off to collect it, believing that some of the fields carrying a heavier crop of weeds than others should be lightly cultivated so the weed seeds could chit and thus be killed when those fields were ploughed. Late in the spring of 1940 the Threshing set had completed its winter programme, the profits were good and as the field officer said, a much heavier programme of threshing could be anticipated during the next winter. Billy and his son had proved good operators, there were very few repairs to be done on the set before it was stored until the Autumn.

The new airfield was almost finished, complete with hangars both large and small, also many Nissen and Romney huts for the airmen, all the time it had been under construction the cafe and the fuel pumps had been busy. Now there was to be petrol rationing and this was, of course, likely to reduce sales considerably, although Harry thought because there was such a large volume of truck sales, it may not make such a difference as a town garage might feel, after all the lorry loads of goods must still be needing to be transported. The summer dragged on and the epic story of Dunkirk was enacted, one day a twin engined aircraft flew into the new airfield, recognised by those who knew about such things as a Wellington bomber, later Hurricane fighters arrived. By August with the harvest in full swing the bombers were in constant use, although the villagers of Jensen soon became used to it and most could sleep through it all. Unfortunately there were always casualties one or two of the Wellingtons failed to return and when this happened the flight crew who often frequented the George in Jensen village would be quiet, at least until spirits were artificially raised by alcohol. The battle of Britain caused some change, more planes were lost, Hurricanes now, until one day two low flying German planes dropped bombs on the airfield and one bomb fell in a cornfield of Johnsons farm, luckily the stooking gang had left, but only by an hour, after this many eyes turned to the sky when an aeroplane was heard. The two German planes also caused the anti aircraft guns to put up a barrage, probably because this was so concentrated it frightened the inhabitants of Jensen more than the bombs.

After the dinner Jenny had with John Patterson, when he had proposed to her, she took the next opportunity to speak with Margy. Margy told her she liked John, but did mother really want to marry again, after all what if she had a baby, Oh well Jenny said, I guess we can avoid that happening, but what did Margy really think. "Well I understand you wanting to marry, she told her, I feel attracted to one of the boys in the garage, but he does not seem to notice me, but I guess I have more time than you, so if you feel you must, just go ahead"."What an independent young lady you are", Jenny told her, Margy rushed over to her mother "Oh mum just do it and be happy, I shall be happy for you". On the Monday John came to the garage, asking Jenny if she had an answer for him, Jenny told him she had, but was he free to go out to dinner that night, "Of course with you ", he told her, so it was arranged they should meet at Jenny's home at seven o'clock. Sitting in the restaurant after the meal Jenny told him she would marry him, in about six months time, meanwhile she considered herself engaged and told him he could stay at the house whenever he was in the district. John produced a ring and slipped it on her finger. Jenny now had a problem, she did not want to dispose of Rob's ring but felt she could not wear it on her left hand, so she asked John if he would mind her wearing it on her other hand, John smiled at her telling her of course he would not mind, she must make her own mind up on that. Later that night they both told Margy of their plans, Margy said she was so happy for them and asked if they wanted her to look for lodgings, so they could have the house to themselves, Margy was soon told not to be so silly, the house was plenty big enough for them all. That night John stayed in the spare bedroom, after a few weeks of that Jenny could stand it no longer and one night she tapped on his bedroom door and climbed into bed with him. Later she just had to tell him how wonderful it was to share a bed with a man again, John confirmed this was his experience and from then on John stayed as often as his duties would allow. About six weeks later Margy asked Jenny if she was sleeping with John, " yes ", Jenny told her, Margy left Jenny in no doubt that she had known, because Jenny was a happier and more carefree person, "does it show so much", Jenny asked," Oh yes all the office staff are speculating about you", Margy told her.

With the battle of Britain almost over, the German air force turned its attention to bombs, luckily Jensen was not attacked but most nights that winter, the anti aircraft guns were in action as the German bombers travelled overhead to attack other places. The air raid sirens would wail and shortly after the characteristic uneven drone of German bombers would worry the inhabitants of Jensen. After a while they became used to this noise, but the sharp ear splitting crack of the anti aircraft guns always made them jump and although they well knew what they were, the sheer noise terrified many of the inhabitants. The air force often held dances in the entertainment hut on the airfield, Johnsons farm supplying various things to the mess would, from time to time get an invitation, sometimes Jay might go, but usually it was Will who would take Joanne. One of the early visits became quite an adventure, Will and Joanne had just left the dance and were on their way home, there had been no air raid warning that night, but about halfway home the guns put up a barrage, Will was riding the BSA slowly because on a dark night and with headlamp masks fitted seeing the road was difficult, the guns took them by surprise, they had heard no sirens to warn them that enemy aircraft were about. In something of a panic he stopped the motor cycle and they both jumped off and as Will laid the machine down they both bolted for the shelter of a big oak tree by the side of the road. Joanne was there first, Will grabbed her and as they both stood shivering with apprehension and shock, the guns went off again, Joanne screamed but Will pulled her to him and kissed her, she returned his kiss with more passion than she had ever shown. "Oh Will I was so frightened she told him Will admitted so was he, but now he was holding her he felt OK. "Just give it a few more minutes then we will go", he told her and then they heard the scream of shrapnel falling, from the exploding shells above, it could be heard hitting the leaves and branches of the tree above them, so arms around one another, lips together they just stayed for a while until they felt there was no more danger. A few minutes grew into twenty, then they climbed on the BSA and Will took her home to Spinney farm, but neither of them would ever forget that night, although they did become accustomed to the guns eventually.

The usual problems now affected almost everyone in Britain, ration books, queuing, shortage of so many things and above all the familiar faces that had been called up for military service, some of the part time ladies who worked when they were needed took permanent jobs and so were lost to Johnsons farm, as were two of the younger members of staff, so Tom realised he would have labour problems in the not too far distant future. Luckily a good percentage of the staff were too old to be called up and Will being the farmers son and working long hours on the farm was exempt, being regarded as an essential worker.

The garage did not fare so well, almost half the staff were taken or volunteered for the war effort and the rest worked seven days a week for long hours to cope with what was still a good business. Eventually the time came for Jenny and John to marry, a quiet wedding in Jensen church and a small family reception at Johnsons farm, Jenny was so pleased to see the Graham family present, David of course working full time on the farm came with them to see his mother married. The Graham family telling Jenny and John how happy they were for them and hoped they would visit together, just as often as Jenny had over the years. There was no time for a honeymoon, but Margy stayed at the farm for a few nights so Jenny and John could have the house to themselves, no housekeeper now, the war effort had taken her away, Jenny and Margy had been sharing the work. Jenny and John shared the master bedroom, the wedding had been held on a Saturday and so they could share a wonderful Saturday night, even if they were in their forties. This was followed by a restful Sunday and another wonderful night, John telling Jenny he had never imagined married life would be so good. Monday morning came and a return to work, Jenny to the garage and John to the Ford factory at Dagenham, Jenny met a smiling Margy, Jenny herself was so happy and Margy just as happy for her. At lunch time Margy was obviously still very happy, so Jenny asked her if the wedding had cheered her up so much, "yes of course mum but another thing is that Pat has come home on leave and asked me to go out with him".

Jensen had settled into a wartime routine, the farm and workers were working longer hours than ever before, it seemed an age ago that the difficult years of the early thirty's had made them all so poor. No enemy action had affected the village other than long periods of anti aircraft fire from the guns on the outlying parts of the air field, obviously firing at aircraft flying over to drop deadly loads of high explosive on other towns and cities, thus many nights sleep were disturbed, but the villagers did not complain. Thus the war dragged on until one day the news on the radio announced that Japan had attacked the American fleet in pearl harbour.

In Iowa USA the Nielsen family heard the news and the heavy losses with disbelief, however it proved to be true, the family consisted of mother, father, two sons and a daughter, they farmed two thousand acres of mixed arable crops, the two sons immediately wanted to rush off and join the armed forces. Jack the father pointed out to them that the war must surely be a short term project, whereas the farm must continue to exist and keep not only the sons, but also their families and hopefully the children from those families. Hank the elder brother was already married, just three months ago, whilst Slim was unmarried and as far as Jack knew, he had not even a girl friend. Jack pointed out that the farm could only spare one son, even then the remaining family would have a big job on hand to meet all the demands of the farm. Jack proud of his Norwegian ancestry but prouder still to call himself an American, felt if anyone should go, and he believed every American family must do its bit for the country, then it should be Slim who volunteered. Hank accepted the logic of Jacks argument with good grace, his new wife being overjoyed not too lose

136

her husband so soon in her marriage. Jack himself had volunteered to serve in the first world war, spending almost a year in the mud and misery of the western front. This experience and the fact that he had seen the air force of the time soaring overhead and out of the misery of trench warfare, caused Jack to insist Slim should join the air force and not the army. Slim listened to this advice, finding when applying to join that his natural fitness and his college qualifications would enable him to enlist as a navigator, so Slim came home to await his call up.

Ten days later his papers arrived along with a travel warrant, reporting for duty he found himself in a hut with twenty four other young men, undergoing basic training. It was hard and degrading, especially for a young man who had never been away from home, his family and his mothers good cooking before. At the end of two weeks he had accustomed himself to the grinding routine of marching, fitness parades and rifle drill with of course the inevitable spit and polish inspections with its harsh punishments for a lack of discipline or quality of presentation. But he survived and could present himself to the folks at home, smart, proud and with five days leave. Reporting to another base, at the end of his leave, he was relieved to find it a large air base with many lecture rooms and not so much physical training, although two mornings each week they were expected to do a ten mile run, however Slim had always been fit and the four weeks basic training had put the finishing touches to a fitness that allowed him to complete these morning runs with little difficulty.

After his arrival at the base there was an introductory day during which the various members of the aircrew were told just what their duties would be, then to the joy of everyone they were introduced to a B17 flying fortress bomber, which was the plane this airfield specialised in training crew to fly. They were told its range carrying capacity and shown the guns which the instructor told them made it almost impossible for a fighter aircraft to shoot it down. At the end of this introduction they were told the next morning, if they wished to continue as flight crew, they must sign an agreement to serve twenty five missions in any war theatre the air force may send them. The training would take four months and then they would gain their wings and report to an operational airfield.

The next morning they all signed and a concentrated training program began, for three months navigators, gunners, pilots etc., trained separately, then for the last month they were set into flight crews. This meant they would take one of the B17 bombers on a dummy mission, be attacked by fighters firing blanks and finally drop bombs on a target in the desert. It was all very realistic but later when they were flying real missions and it was freezing cold, noisy and terrifying, these exercises were seen as little more than acting out a war and not at all real. Nevertheless the final months training had bonded the crew together and that meant as far as possible, that crew stayed together, at least in the early days of wartime missions.

Two weeks leave at home and a train journey to an airfield near Boston, where Slim joined up with the flight crew and were allocated a new flying fortress, a couple of shake down flights and they were ready to fly the atlantic. The flight plan took them to a place called Jensen airbase, Slim was well prepared and confident he could bring the bomber in with no trouble. Back in Jensen the rumours of the airfield being vacated by the RAF were circulating, against much disbelief from the villagers. However one morning the RAF planes flew away and by late afternoon the whole village could feel the sense of desolation emanating from the airfield, even the lorries and staff cars had left.

The next day an American jeep led a convoy of lorries driven by a mixed bag of white and black men, they drew into the airfield complex and began to unload. This went on for a week, at the end of the second week a new noise was obvious, no longer the smooth sound of Rolls Royce Merlin engines, but a much harsher sound from the four radial air cooled engines of a flying fortress bomber. To be followed by eight more in quick succession. Two nights later the George was invaded by American airmen, in beautifully cut uniforms and talking with strange accents, they soon drank the pub dry and upon being told no more supplies would be coming until next week, two of them returned to the base and brought a jeep loaded with beer in crates and bottles of both rye and scotch whiskey. The proprietor of the George allowed them to consume the drink on the premises and a precedent was set. The locals also enjoyed this bountiful supply, no booze in the pub and the Americans brought their own, but if the George had supplies the they would drink whilst it lasted.

Two weeks later twelve bombers left Jensen airbase to rendevous with others and start a concentrated daylight attack on Germany. None of the aircrew had any fear of being shot down, after all they had been told these bombers had the best defence of any that had ever flown. An underbelly gun, two forward firing guns, one each side the fuselage and a tail gunner, the bombers could, in theory, defend themselves from any angle a fighter plane might approach from. This daylight raid on Bremen, one of the heavily defended German cities, brought home to these new aircrew just what they were up against, especially when only nine bombers returned. Three planes and fifty one airmen lost on their first mission, flying a different formation and flying much higher meant they were better defended on subsequent missions, but still the odd plane did not return, a much too frequent happening as far as these airmen were concerned. It was to this situation that Slim brought flying fortress "Spirit of the west" to Jensen, a new and green crew came to join Europes war. The air crews already feeling like veterans, tried to instruct the newcomers in the problems they must face, there were four new bombers and the station commander decided to add only two of them to the next mission, being hopeful they might quickly learn from their much more experienced colleagues.

They had instilled into them, to fly in box formation as a better defence against fighters, if they flew into cloud never to vary from the position they held or there was a great danger of collision and when the bombs were gone, climb as quickly as possible, as high as possible and high tail it for home. Very few of the German fighters could operate at the height a fortress could, when it was not carrying bombs. For this first mission, Slim had his papers and maps with the target and flight path marked, it was again Bremen. There was much nervousness as they climbed into the bomber and tested their various intercom facilities and oxygen supply. The captain started the engines, with their characteristic hit and miss firing and much smoke until they had run for some seconds, then with the four engines running sweetly they joined the line of planes waiting to take off. All the crew were, of course, nervous even Slim found a knot in his stomach but he at least, had to keep check on the lead bombers navigation and be able to tell the captain just where their position was at any time he might ask. As they approached Germany a barrage of anti aircraft fire met them, by this time the captain had ordered oxygen masks to be worn and the gun crews to attach their safety harness, all so different to the exercises they had carried out back home.

Slim from his position behind the two pilots could see the puffs of bursting shells and on one occasion, even felt the plane bounce in sympathy with a near miss. Then the fighters came, although he could not see them the guns on board, Spirit of the west, made a deafening noise. Eventually they came to the target, the plane ran in smoothly and released the bombs, immediately circling away from the target and climbing under full power, at maximum height the captain asked for a course home. Slim, hoping against hope he had it correct, gave it to him and they all settled down for the long flight. Some anti aircraft fire and three fighters attacked them, but no damage was done, thus the new crew survived their first raid, the other new crew also returned as did all the other planes, so for once there were no losses. This situation did not last over the next few months, many crews were lost, replacements were of course always sent but it was a fearful time for them all, Slim amongst them. Spirit of the west had several near misses, once returning with half the tail shot away and once on only three engines due to cannon fire from a fighter, but the crew considered themselves lucky to survive so long, although they were always aware that the next mission may be their last. They found the worst part was at night, perhaps the night before a mission when often sleep was difficult to find and a heavy feeling lay in the pit of the stomach.

Will was now a regular visitor to Spinney farm and Joanne also came to Johnsons farm, but by June they were both very busy in the hay harvest and most nights they did not meet. But as soon as the harvest slackened, Will was round to see if Joanne was free to go for a spin on the BSA., Jay, although a year older than Will had no boy friends, or even anyone to escort her out in the evenings. Her cousin Margy, now having an arrangement with Pat, the boy from the garage, now in the RAF, would often accompany Jay to a dance or cinema, but the demand of the farm and garage severely curtailed their excursions together.

Joe Johnson, now 72 years old could feel himself, not just slowing down, but also losing strength, he no longer loaded the hay or corn waggons. Although Jane still ferried them between field and stack, Joe now was relegated to walking around the farmyard, doing odd carpentry jobs and taking meals to the field workers. Joe also left his bed later in the mornings unless he had arranged to take the milk to the station, that was still Merri's job unless she asked Joe to stand in for her.

The American aircrew on Jensen field were by now, early July, a close knitted community, they were often found drinking and gambling together, Slim joined in this to some extent, but preferred to take a long country walk, finding the English countryside so different to that of his home state of Iowa. He was nevertheless a close member of the flight crew and when the captain returned from a twenty four

142

stayed at, with a girl from Staunton, would provide a room permanently booked to the flight crew, for a ridiculously low price per night. They should all contribute to a kitty and have some place quiet and secluded where they could go, with or without a girl, when they could get away from the airbase.

The corn harvest started on Johnsons farm in the middle of July, but the labour situation was bad, however Jay told her dad she believed that she could cut the fifteen acres of wheat alongside the trunk road, without anyone riding the binder, because it was such an even crop. With the hay harvest not finally finished Tom had little option but to agree, thus it was that having a broken twine, the wartime twine for tying the sheaves was pretty awful quality, Jay was just re-threading the needle when an American voice said "hey little girl, let me help you there". Jay looking up, saw an American uniform standing by the binder and a voice telling her "we have a binder like that at home". Smiling back at him Jay said " I think I have done it now thank you", the American went on to ask her where the binder operator was and was soon told she was managing on her own because they were so short of labour. " Gee I could ride that for you, I have ridden thousands of acres back home, we have a farm just run by our family". Jay agreed to Slim, for that was who it was, riding the binder for her and when the stooking gang came and Merri with a meal, they sat down together. Slim soon told Merri he was enjoying himself and could he do some more with Jay, he was also very complimentary about the food, as he told them, it was almost a year since he had tasted genuine home bake.

That evening Slim was invited into the kitchen for a meal,

the binder sheeted up and the Fordson in its shed. During the meal Slim told them of his home and how he had come to be in the air force,"I guess my dad got it wrong when he told me to be an airman because it was safer than the army", so obviously you are flight crew, Joe said. Slim told them he was a navigator and had completed thirteen missions over Germany but was not flying this week, they were having a break whilst Spirit of the west was having new engines fitted and some bodywork repairs caused by anti aircraft fire. Some of the crew had gone to London, others were just taking it easy and gambling a little, Slim offered to to come again if they would feed him like this, he had four days left yet. Jay asked him if he could stay on the farm, obviously some of the crew were sleeping away so could he?," sure, but I must let the gate know where I am", Jay soon told him they had some spare rooms and volunteered to run him to the airfield to report and collect anything he might need. They set off for the airfield in Jay's Austin, Merri looked at Tom, asking what he thought to that, Tom laughed, telling her he reckoned Jay was smitten with the American. Three days later they knew much more about Slim, about his home and their farm, they also had some idea of how hard and dangerous was the flying he did. Meanwhile Jay and Slim were cutting corn and walking out in the evenings when the days work was done, this prompted Merri to caution her daughter about getting too involved with the American, Jay replied she knew it was unwise but could not help herself, but assured her mother she would try and not become too involved.

On the fourth day Slim returned to the airfield, they all missed his happy character, but non more so than Jay. The next morning Jay was cutting corn on John Deane's farm and Joanne was riding the binder, Johnsons farm had always cut the Deane's corn, when she became aware of aircraft noise, the Americans were going on a mission. Jay stopped the tractor whilst she counted twelve fortresses take off. At the end of the cutting day, the first of the planes could be seen approaching the runway and with some relief Jay counted twelve returning over the next twenty minutes. Later with the binder covered over for the night, Jay drove the tractor home, dropping Joanne off at Spinney farm on the way. Jay put the tractor in the shed and rushed to the kitchen, asking her mum if Slim had telephoned yet, obviously disappointed Jay told Merri she would have a bath, but be sure to shout her if Slim called. An hour later and with Jay fussing about in the kitchen, the telephone rang, she rushed over to it and heard Slim's voice, telling her he was back and could he come to visit, I will fetch you he was told. So Slim was again in the kitchen sitting round the old scrubbed table taking a late meal, as all the family assembled after a hard days harvesting.

Tom asked Slim what his trip was like and where he had been, if he was allowed to tell them. Sure I can tell you, Hamburg was the destination, but the defences are getting pretty bad, anti aircraft fire especially, we had quite a grilling part of a wing tip shot off and one engine put out of action by machine gun fire from a fighter, but one of our centre gunners is claiming a kill on that one. But we are out of action now for several days, so I can come back harvesting if you like. I will run you back to camp for your work clothes Jay told him, Slim looked at Merri, is it OK that I stay here ma'am, I do not want to take advantage of your kindness. Merri looked at him saying she did not mind and even if she did, Jay would probably win any argument. So

Slim, with a sleeping out pass and the farm telephone number held with security at the gatehouse, took up residence again in Johnsons farm. After only two days the telephone rang that evening, with a message for Slim, would he report for duty as soon as possible. Jay took him to the airfield, the little Austin was now recognised and Jay was allowed to run him into the camp, Jay was so sad but realised nothing could be done, left him, but not before they shared a long affectionate kiss.

Returning to the farm she sat silently in the kitchen on a chair, such a different girl to the one of an hour or so ago. Joe and Jane had retired to bed, Tom already climbing the stairs, when Merri, looking across to Jay said very gently, "Jay you are becoming too involved with Slim", "yes I know but I am so happy when he is here and I feel so low when he has to leave, now I am worried he will fly again tomorrow and I may never see him again", Merri explained that was fate, she understood her daughters feelings and would not oppose them, but did point out to Jay she had little experience of boyfriends and might it not be a passing fancy. Jay left her in no doubt that she felt it too deeply for that and felt sure she had fallen in love with Slim. Jay explained to her mother she must not interfere, Jay feeling she could work it out for herself. Merri asked Jay to tell her if she had any problems, after all I am your mother and I do want you to be happy, but you must prepare yourself for Slim perhaps telling you he has a girl friend, or even a wife, back home. Or, heaven forbid, he may not return from a mission, so you must always have in your mind to enjoy his company but beware of disaster happening. The next morning Jay was back to her cheerful self, telling her mum that she had thought it through and decided she must enjoy

Slim whilst he was here and leave the future to look after itself. Jay took her tractor to the field but watched carefully for the planes to take off, to her surprise the airfield remained silent. Three days later Jay received a letter, over stamped USAF, it was from Slim, telling her he was at a training establishment and training for a special mission, but he had been told it would be safer than those he had been flying, he would telephone her as soon as he returned.

CHAPTER SIX

Dark war years

Jenny was now settled into a new life with John, she was deeper in love with him than when they were married and their love life was blooming, although now in her mid forties Jenny was only too well aware that she could still become pregnant, neither John or Jenny wanted this to happen, but on occasions Jenny, feeling it to be safe, made love without the protectives John always had available. On one occassion they had actually made love naturally when Jenny calculated, afterwards, they should not have done so. The garage was still making good profits, partly because the wage bill was reduced with staff having left to join the forces and partly due to new vehicles being scarce, the old ones were being serviced at regular intervals and, of course, because they were older, needing more repairs. The depot., on the trunk road was also producing profits, petrol and diesel sales were holding up well, although private motoring was in decline due to petrol rationing, the lorries still mostly using petrol, were hardly decreasing in volume. Again these were getting older and needing more repairs, just as were the tractors being serviced by the trunk road depot.

The airfield across the road did not bring in much business, it was almost self supporting, but a few officers had become regular visitors to the tea rooms, although restricted by rationing. It was not unknown for Johnsons farm to provide something, eggs, ham, pork or milk, to bolster these rations, whilst still using finely ground flour, two ladies from the village were still making apple pies, or other fruit in season, thus the incentive for lorry drivers to call and fill up both their trucks and themselves was quite strong.

It took two whole weeks for Slim to return to Jensen, Jay had almost given up hope of hearing from him again, but had put a good face on it and carried on with the tractor work day after day. Then suddenly there he was again, his so well remembered voice on the telephone, Jays heart jumped, her face broke into a smile as she arranged to meet him at the camp gate in ten minutes. Slim climbed into the Austin, turned to Jay and kissed her, then he told her he only had four hours, but felt he should spend part of it with the family, then perhaps they could have a couple of hours to themselves. Arriving back at Johnsons farm, tea was almost over but Slim and Jay sat down at the table with the rest of the family. All were curious to know where Slim had been, he told them he had been on a navigators training course, they were about to start nightime raids from Jensen and all the crew had been training. All they now had to do was a few dummy runs and then they would be operational again. "Oh dear that means it will be more dangerous", Jay said, Slim told them all, that the command had decided day light losses were too heavy to carry and that night raids would be safer, being much more difficult to spot in the dark skies, especially with our camouflage paint. Jay decided if they were going out she must go and change, this gave Slim the opportunity to ask Tom and Merri if they had any objection to Jay going out with him, both replied they had no serious objections, but felt Jay was becoming far too attached to him, after all, as they pointed out he would, at some stage return to his own country,

149

leaving Jay both sad and very upset. Slim smiled, as he felt about her right now, they were told, he wanted to ask her to be his wife and had already written and told his family about her. He then went on to say he had to face facts, he had nine more missions to do before he would return to America. Even the next flight might be his last and although he knew Jay would be devastated he felt she would eventually recover. He did not wish to leave a young widow in England, even though he felt confident he could avoid having a family. Perhaps after a few more flights he may wish to ask their permission for Jay to become engaged to him, but he would not consider marriage until he had finished flying. Merri thanked him for being so frank with them, telling him she already knew Jay was committed to a relationship with him and felt powerless to stop it, so she just hoped it would work out alright for all of them. At this stage Jay came into the kitchen, no longer in work clothes but now dressed in a moderately short skirt, white blouse and silk stockings, saying "come on yank we have only two hours left".

After they had gone Tom and Merri looked at one another, both realising there was no turning back now. Merri saying she was glad about his responsibility of not having children before he finished flying, she was sure they would find the opportunity to sleep together before long and suspected Jay would be the instigator of that situation. The Austin travelled about four miles, then turned into a track through a wood and pulled over between the trees, out of sight to anyone travelling the trunk road. Jay climbed out of the car and from the back seat took a rug, which she spread out by a rear wheel, for just a moment they both sat in silence. "What were my parents saying whilst I was out of the room", Jay asked, Slim told her most of the conversation. Jay told him she was certain she loved him, but did he love her or was he just lonely, "oh no it is much deeper than that, I know we are in love, but we cannot proceed along the way I am sure we both want, until I have done all my twenty five missions", Slim told her. Jay immediately argued that they could and indeed, should, every moment being precious to them, but Slim was adamant, no engagement or marriage until his flying duties were over. Slim insisted it was one thing to leave a broken hearted young girl, who would eventually recover, but quite another to leave a young widow. Soon they had arms around one another and were sharing loving kisses, after a while Slim told Jay if she wanted they could share the bedroom in the village pub that the crew of Spirit of the west jointly paid for. Jay must not think he was pressuring her into anything, so he would leave that decision to her, but she must consider the feelings of her parents, allowing him to be present when they were told if she decided that was what she wanted to do. "Slim, I am twenty three years old and I do not have to ask my parents permission to sleep with the man I love", but Slim was adamant they must be told, so an agreement was reached that after his flying duties were finished they should be married. "Slim I hate to argue with you but what if I have a baby, surely a widow with a baby would be better than an unmarried mother, especially if the father was an American", Slim told Jay not to worry about such a thing, he would make sure she did not have a baby.

Later as they lay together on the rug, Slim bending over Jay, his lips on hers, his tongue exploring her mouth, he put his hand on the tempting part of her thigh and lifting his head, he asked her if she realised he had never seen her dressed as a girl before. "Is it an improvement", he was asked, "Gee sure is, but I fell in love with a working girl, this is a bonus tonight". Later in the dusk, Jay lay with her skirt round her waist, Slim's hand on her stomach, "Oh Slim go on, go further ", Jay implored, "no not tonight, I am not prepared, but from now on I will always be prepared". The next morning Jay came down to the kitchen with a smile on her face, Merri looking at her saying I guess from your smile that last night went well, Jay left her in no doubt that it had, but unfortunately she would not see Slim for about a week. He was to do two night flights to other aerodromes and then take his first operational night flight.

The corn harvest was almost finished, Will and Jay were now concentrating on the Autumn cultivations. Johnsons farm had a record harvest, but it had been such a hard one to gather, with the shortage of labour, luckily there had been a full moon at the peak of the carrying time and the lack of evening dew had enabled almost a week of extra hours being worked, on two occasions they had worked until midnight. The threshing set had now started its winter work, Billy still travelled with it but now his son Jacky was the main worker, Tom was still looking out for a replacement for Billy. Tom also had to think about a replacement for Josie, now sixty four years old, still looking after the poultry, with the help of a lady from the village. It was the same story at the garage, long hours, especially for Bertie, but luckily he had developed a friendship for John Patterson who had taken to helping Bertie with the planning and paperwork of the service department. Margy was now working closely with Jenny and had a desk in her office, much to Jenny's pleasure Margy had become part of Jenny and John's family, going most places together unless Pat was home on leave, when Margy was rarely seen. Pat had been the foreman under Bertie, before joining the RAF. and was now working on Spitfires at an airfield about 100 miles away.

Johnsons farm now had the roots to harvest but this was made much easier by the War Ag. field officers offer of a gang of Italian prisoners of war, this Tom gratefully accepted and set them to start the sugar beet harvest. Joe and Tom worked with them for the first morning, just to show them the way they wanted the job done, then leaving them to work alone, but visited quite often to see all was well. There were thirty Italians and although they worked slowly it was surprising how well the job was going, the kitchen lady and Merri, sometimes Jane always baked a pie for them, the farm was allowed extra rations at harvest time, Joe always took the pie to them at midday, this gave him the opportunity to check on their work.

Jane had told them in one of the evening meetings that Johnsons farm was doing well and she felt that two thousand pounds should be invested in a longer term investment than the current account, which paid no interest. Even so they would still have almost two thousand pounds in the bank and all the wheat still to thresh. Tom said he would apply for a permit to buy two new Fordson tractors, but of course he did not know if the permits would be forthcoming or even if tractors were available.

The day after Jay and Slim had been together in the wood, Jay worked late in one of the stubble fields, the moon was just setting as she set off for home. Then she heard the unmistakable sound of a flying fortress taking off, she was surprised to see the airfield lit up, then realised it was the runway lights. The twelve bombers smoothly left the ground, even Jay could recognise they were not loaded and so she had little concern for Slim. The next morning, before it was light they returned and again on the following night, as far as Jay could count they all returned safely. Two nights later she heard the engines start again, Jay had put her tractor in the shed and was walking across the horse yard towards the house when the first, hesitant and rough sounding engine started. Jay turned and walked through the mixing place, where the cattle food was mixed, and across the stackyard, through the gate at the far end which led to a grass field. Here she stood, more and more engines started and eventually the initial roughness settled down to a smooth steady beat.

Then the landing lights came on, it seemed the whole country side was lit up, Jay could see the shapes of the planes silhouetted as they taxied to the take off stations. As the first flying fortress reached the runway end a heavy roar, that blotted out the sound of those still taxying into position, announced it was taking off, Jay could see it gathering speed down the runway. Jay knew at once this was for real, not like the other two she had seen in the darkness when the planes rose into the air halfway down the runway. Tonight there was a heavier note to the engines and it was well toward the end of the runway before Jay saw the outline of the plane rise over the high hedge and disappear into the night sky. Jay counted twelve planes, saying a mental prayer for Slim and all the crews, flying off into the unknown, some perhaps never to return, leaving broken hearted girls or wives behind in a far distant land. Jay returned to the house ready for the evening meal, although the departure of the planes had taken her appetite away. Afterwards Tom, Merri, Jane and Joe sat in the office, Jay sat with them, Will as usual had gone to the Deane's farm to see Joanne. Tom looked at Jay, saying "they have all gone then", Jay told them that they had, all twelve of them. Merri looked across at Jay, telling her not too worry, she felt sure they would all come back safely,"Oh mum how can you say that, they are even now crossing the sea and beginning to fly into flak and hostile aircraft, it is one big gamble if they come back at all". Merri could see Jay was almost in tears, after recovering for a few moments Jay told them Slim had told her he wanted to marry her, but not until his flying missions were over, he had eight more after tonight. Jay also decided to tell them of the room at the distant pub that the flight crew kept on permanent reservation and how she had decided she would go there with Slim, so at least, if she lost him she would have some memories to treasure. "Oh Jay, do you have to be so loose", Merri asked, "mother it is not loose to go with the man you love in these circumstances", Jay insisted, Jane butted in, saying "Merri leave her alone, I understand her need, as I am sure you do if you stop and think", "well yes, I do but still it seems wrong to me". Tom smiled at Jay saying "your mum had different ideas to the ones she has now, before we were married, so you go ahead and enjoy yourself, I believe we can trust Slim to do the correct thing".

Joe told them the sugar beet was finished and carted into a heap ready for the two lorries who had contracted to cart it to the factory, there was no permit available to Johnsons farm from the beet factory to ship any beet until next week, but the contractor had spare permits to take sixteen tons this week. Joe had told him to telephone when he would come, so they could put some of the Italians to help load it. "It will probably be a record crop", Joe told them, but of

155

course he could not say how the sugar content would work out until the first samples were analysed at the factory, so they would not know exactly what the return would be until that had been done.

Jay lay in bed that night unable to sleep, until about half past three she heard the noise of an approaching plane, quickly leaving her bed she rushed upstairs to the small bedrooms, now unoccupied, where the servants used to sleep. Taking up a position by a window where she could see the distant airfield she saw the landing lights come on, the first bomber touched down and then taxied towards the storage area. Over the next half hour ten planes landed, but then the lights were extinguished. Jay was desolate, feeling certain Slim was missing, she sat there for another hour but no more planes came, Jay returned to her bed and cried herself to sleep. The next morning Jay, with a heavy heart, greased her tractor, filled it with fuel, checked the oil and returned to the kitchen for breakfast. Just a cup of tea please, she told Jessie, the village lady now helping in the kitchen, "now Jay you cannot live on tea", Jessie told her,"Oh I cannot eat this morning ", Jay replied. As she finished her tea, the phone rang, Jay rushed over and picked it up, to hear Slim's voice say "Hi honey", Jay could not reply for a moment, then cried "Oh Slim is it really you I was so miserable when only ten planes came back", Slim told her he was going to bed but would be over at teatime. Jay returned to the table, telling Jessie she could eat her breakfast now.

After her days ploughing, Jay was anxious to return to the farm, but being a responsible girl, resisted the temptation to knock off early, finally she returned to the farm and put her tractor in the shed, as she did so a jeep made a complete circle in the horse yard and put Slim off, complete with his night bag. Jay ran over to him and throwing her arms round his neck kissed him with some passion. Later at the tea table Slim told them that the last night was the most terrifying of his life, they had set off to Hamburg, but taken a new course over the north sea and down the side of Denmark, he had no trouble navigating but as they approached land, there was intermittent cloud cover. Going through one of these clouds the bomber gave a terrible judder and coming out the other side they could see the right hand wing tip was missing. They came to the conclusion that they had collided with another plane, but luckily it had not damaged the control system. When they were in clear sky again, Jed the captain, had decided to break radio silence and tell the rest of the flight to open out a little because of the collision. Looking across to the bomber on their right they could see damage to his wing and concluded that was the plane they had collided with.

After this they flew through several clouds, without any more difficulty, but about fifty miles from target they flew into an extra large cloud. It was really thick and Jed had said, I am trying to maintain station but have no idea if I am succeeding. As they broke clear, a planes tail loomed up in front of them, Jed shut down his engines, luckily they were flying at the bottom rear of the box so he had no fear of hitting another plane flying into them from the rear. The plane in front of them, in almost a split second, seemed to rise, or as Slim said, maybe they decended as Jed shut the throttles. In any case there was a terrible crash, flames and sparks, as the plane in front, hit the one above. As they both dropped from view Jed told them he could see, just for a second, one plane dropping away with all four propellers broken and a piece of wing missing, the plane above dived across the front of them with severe tail damage. Slim shivered as he finished his tale, saying he guessed they had been a split second from death.

Whilst Slim had been recounting this story, they all realised they had stopped eating, "Oh well I guess we live to fight another day", he said as they again continued with their tea. After tea Slim told them he would not be flying again for five days, it would take that time to repair the planes and assess this first night operation. He hesitantly asked if Jay could go with him the next night, Friday and stay over Saturday night, at a pub where the flight crew had a permanent room. Jay told him she had explained to her family about this plan already and the answer was yes. After tea Jay and Slim walked over the farm until they came to a natural arbour in a high hedge, by the pheasant rearing spinney, sitting on a bed of dry leaves they were soon kissing with tremendous affection, then Jay asked how frightened had Slim really been. Terrified he told her, at one time I never thought I would see you again, worst of all now, so many of my friends are gone and I feel I shall never see them again. As they lay on the dry leaves Jay asked Slim to undress her, she undid the buttons on his uniform and they were soon totally naked. Jay could feel excitement rising in her loins, whilst Slim was erect and willing. Jay wriggled towards him, pulling his head down so she could kiss his lips, whilst Slim held one breast and gently slid his hand up the inside of her thigh. Stop Slim told her, I must use a pro-kit or you may have a baby, no Slim not tonight, it is most unlikely, but maybe tomorrow we will use a kit. A few more minutes and both of them lost all thoughts of responsibility, Slim slipping inside Jay who immediately responded with passion. Eventually as they lay together, Slim told her he had promised her parents she would not have a baby until they were married. "Oh it is most unlikely I shall have a baby at this time of the month", Jay told him, or indeed even this week end, but perhaps it would be wise if you wish, to use a protective next time.

Jay took her work on the farm seriously, even though Slim was staying at the farm, she left to do a days ploughing on the Friday before Slim was awake, believing his need of sleep was a priority. Jay and Will were ploughing in the same field and during one of their breaks Will asked Jay, if she thought Joanne might be having a baby, she had told him her monthly period was two weeks overdue. "What have you done towards it, do you have a guilty conscience", yes Will told her,"three times since the harvest I have thought we should not have gone so far". "Just what I thought last night", Jay told him, " go and tell mum she will understand, will Joanne's parents, but I am sure Joanne must tell her mum herself". That night with the tractor put away and Jay bathed and changed out of her working clothes, she drove Slim away from Johnsons farm, but not before Merri had taken Slim's hands in her own and asked him, very seriously, to look after her daughter.

The journey to the pub where they intended to stay, passed off without incident, they were shown to an upstairs bedroom with a bathroom attached, itself unusual for a country pub. The room overlooked fields at the rear, with some young stock grazing and a field of mangolds half harvested. Later having had a good dinner and a sit in the bar, they retired to their room, as Slim hung up his uniform he removed from his pocket a blue and white packet with "Pro-kit" written across it. The contents were described as a protective, always to be used to avoid contracting any disease, a warning to use it only once and never be tempted to enter a woman without it in place. There was also a small sealed packet of lubricant and an antiseptic wipe. Jay looked at this, saying "how impersonal and scientific, is that really how the American forces see love?", "no Slim told her, it is just that they suspect most of the personnel will go with the first available female and will know nothing about her".

By this time Jay was undressed, as was Slim, they climbed into the comfortable bed and enjoyed the foreplay they had enjoyed the previous night. Slim eased away from Jay for a moment and slipped on the protective, Jay was about to object until she thought how Slim has assured her mother that Jay would come to no harm with him. Jay decided she did not want to embarrass him, so she held her peace, thinking of what Will had told her that morning and decided she and Slim must act more responsibly. That night Slim and Jay learned a great deal about one another, in truth neither were very experienced lovers but the act of learning was sufficient to release a great deal of passion and so that weekend became one they would never forget. Both came home on Sunday afternoon, happy and satisfied, Slim returned to the airbase and Jay prepared for another weeks work. She found the opportunity to speak with Will, asking what news he had of Joanne, nothing more Jay was told. Late on Sunday evening Merri came into Jay's room, asking her if the weekend had gone well and was she certain she knew the dates when it was safe to make love. Jay assured her she had not forgotten the wise words her mother had given her, what now, seemed so long ago, but assured her mother Slim had taken care of her, although it

160

might be more important to take care over the next few days. Then Jay could not help herself, but to say, to Merri, "it is not me you should be worrying about but Will", Merri looked at her, asking, Will and Joanne, possibly Jay told her but I think it is already too late.

Two things happened on the Tuesday night, Jay again watched the fully loaded planes take off, this time with two untried crews, newly flown in from America and Merri found Will and Joanne arrive for tea. After tea Merri asked them to come into the sitting room for a moment. As they sat together, Merri asked them if they had anything to tell her, looking at Joanne she asked if she had a secret worry, because she had lost her sparkle and looked worried. Joanne's eyes filled with tears as she said in a halting low voice, "Mrs. Johnson I have not had a period for almost seven weeks now". Merri looked at her and asked if she had told her mother, suggesting she should do so, perhaps this very night and take Will with her, it was obviously partly his problem anyway, "Oh and from now on you had better call me mum, like my own children do". Will and Joanne departed to the Deane's farm and Merri walked into the office, "what was that all about", Tom asked, Merri told him perhaps he had better get used to the idea of becoming a grandfather. The next morning at four o'clock Jay found herself again sitting by the window counting the planes as they returned, but this time there were twelve. Over the next two weeks there were two more operations without further loss, Slim always telephoning her as soon as the debriefing was over, usually about seven thirty. He could not leave the airfield, but after the third operational flight he was able to tell Jay they had plane damage and he would be over at teatime when he had been to bed.

Jay walked into the kitchen after putting her tractor away, to find Slim hunched in a chair by the fire, looking obviously older and and with none of the usual colour in his cheeks. Merri and Jessie had given him a drink, but it remained untouched. Merri looked at Jay, indicating to her to try and talk to him, drawing up a chair to his side, Jay said gently "come on Slim, tell me what is troubling you". He looked at her with a weak smile, "Oh I guess it will wear off, we got shot up pretty bad last night". "Tell me about it", Jay demanded, Slim told her they had been to bomb Dusseldorf, which of course, meant a long journey over land . They had gone through heavy flak over the target and approaching it, after the bombs were released they had turned away from the target, but because so many planes were involved had been unable to climb quickly as they were used to doing. They had to hold station until they were about ten miles from the target area before they could climb, about half way to the climb point they had again come under very heavy anti aircraft fire and in an instant had almost received a direct hit. It must have been very close, because the right hand side centre gunner had been blown away from his gun, a large piece of the fuselage had also been blown away. Luckily the damage, which was heavy, was above the controls running to the tail, or he would not be sitting here now.

The bang and subsequent wind noise from the hole in the fuselage was deafening and then as they became accustomed to it there was a terrible screaming that Slim admitted chilled his blood. The screaming was Jess, the centre gunner, not only had he been blown away from his gun, but when he came round he realised his arm was blown away just above the elbow. The flight engineer, who

162

had received some simple first aid training was despatched to see what he could do. Cutting off the gunners surplus clothing he put a tourniquet on the arm to stop the bleeding. The engineer then injected Jess with morphine, after this they had climbed slowly to their return flight height, Jed the captain had asked Slim to go and see how the engineer was getting on. Slim found Jess the gunner, laid on the floor, now almost unconscious and very quiet, the two men managed to wrap him in blankets, it was desperately cold, especially with the air rushing through the gaping hole in the plane. Then Slim said he saw it, the severed arm lying on the floor by the missing piece of fuselage, Slim told Jay he guessed it must have been the shock, but he just grabbed it and threw it through the hole. Returning to his navigators position he found he was trembling, however they got the plane back and the gunner away to hospital. Looking at Spirit of the west, he wondered how Jed had managed to fly it home, the right hand side of the plane was riddled with small holes and the tall tail had its tip blown off, it also was full of small holes. After the debriefing Slim had felt better, especially when told the hospital had said Jess would recover, but of course he would not fly again. Going to bed Slim had difficulty going to sleep, but must have gone off eventually, but then he had found himself sitting up in bed, shouting "don't let it go through that hole", sweating heavily and trembling. Jay sat quietly with him, putting her arm round him she told him to come for a walk, whilst mum sets the tea table for tea. After tea Slim gave them an account of his flight, Jay encouraged him to do this, thinking the more times he told the story the better it would be for him. About ten o'clock they all retired to bed, Slim saying he was ready, not having slept well during the day.

saying he was ready, not having slept well during the day. About two in the morning, Jay was awakened by a scream and someone shouting "no, don't let it get out, grab it". Jay ran to Slims room, he was sitting up in bed obviously sweating but without colour in his face. Tom and Merri came to the door, by this time Slim was standing up, Jay holding his hand, "gee I am sorry to have woken you all, I guess I had better sleep on the base tomorrow". Jay walked to her room and put on her housecoat, whilst Tom and Merri walked back to theirs, as Jay passed them on the landing she told them he would not disturb them again, turning into Slim's room she shut the door.

The night Will and Joanne set off to see Joanne's mother and father, they were both very apprehensive, arriving at the Deane's farm they walked inside to find John and Jo with Janette having a last drink before bed. They sat down with them and Joanne, now having built herself up into a high state of tension, said "mum I think I am having a baby". Silence reigned for just a second or so and then Jo asked if Joanne was sure, "no but I have not had a period for nearly seven weeks", Joanne told her. Jo turned to Will asking if he was responsible, Will swallowed hard and admitted he was. "Are you intending to marry", John asked, When being told they were, John's response was that he was pleased to find at least some sign of responsibility, but he let them know he was disgusted with their behaviour.

Janette then turned to John saying he should be pleased, first because they were both old enough to have a family, second because Joanne had such a good boy to become her husband and then told him that she had found herself in that position with Johns dad, so it was not such an unusual occurrence. By this time some of the shock was wearing off, John laughed "Oh well I guess it runs in the family then", he told them, Jo asked if they wanted a drink and as they sat with a cup in their hands, asked if they had made any plans, on being told no she suggested they talk about it the next day, when they all had time to sleep on the problem. A little later Will returned home to find Merri waiting to see how he had gone on and asking what Jo's reaction was, "they were not too pleased but we parted friends", Will told her.

The morning after Jay had entered Slim's room, she was up at her usual time and Slim followed her into the kitchen. During breakfast he again said how sorry he was for disturbing their night and again offered to go back to the base to sleep. He was told not to be so silly, the nightmare would probably never return. Towards the end of breakfast Jay asked her dad if he could get one of the old Irish Fordsons going, because Slim could do some top cultivations and the fresh air might relax his nerves, Jay realised how terribly stressful Slims flying hours were. By lunchtime Slim was happily harrowing in the next field to the one Jay was ploughing. That night as they climbed the beautiful main staircase, Merri just had time to see Jay turn into Slim's room as she closed her door.

The day after Will and Joanne had broken the news to the Deane family, Jo had spoken to Joanne, telling her she should have been more careful, but Joanne said she had never intended to go so far, it just happened, they decided that it was better that Joanne carried on as normal for now and Jo would talk to Merri about what was best to do later. That morning Merri called at the Deane's on her way back from delivering the milk to the dairy in Little Staunton. She was made welcome and a cup of tea was soon provided, both Jo and Janette were present. Merri said "you know why I have called today", Jo told her she did, what did Merri think about the situation the children had created. Merri told Jo she wished it were different, but overnight she had discussed it with Tom and they had decided, the present situation included, that they could not wish for a better match for their only son. Then Merri asked could they accept Will as a son in law, "Oh Merri, we accept him as a son", Jo told her, Thus it was agreed that they should marry the next month in Jensen church and after a honeymoon, Joanne and Will should live at Johnsons farm.

After three days on the Fordson, Slim returned to the airbase and Jay returned to sleep in her own room. The first night she had slept with Slim, when they had both slept in each others arms, as Jay thought to sooth Slims terrible dream, the next night they had enjoyed a wonderful love life, Jay being sure she would not now become pregnant, the familiar Pro-kit remained unused. Good food fresh air and above all, Jays love, seemed to make a new man of Slim, he returned to duty seeming to be his old self, as he told Jay, only five more missions and I have finished operations for ever. Two nights after Slim's departure, Jay was again counting the planes as they took off and in the early hours of the morning counting them back again, but she did not sleep afterwards, only eleven returned. Slim telephoned that morning as usual, telling her he was OK but could not leave the base.

Jay suffered two more nights of worry but each morning Slim telephoned and her worries were dispelled. The next break he had was for almost a week, so they decided to visit the coast, Jay had found that Slim had never seen the sea, only by flying over it. During this break he told Jenny he had been to see his commander and set the wheels in motion to marry after his tour of operations was completed. He also told her he had written to his mother and told her how Jay and her family had helped him during his recent difficulties. The break spent on the East coast was one of constant surprise to Jay, she was amazed at the hundreds of American flyers in town, she learned to dance the jitterbug, she was in awe of the night sky, filled with bombers until the very air shivered with their noise, but most of all and very precious, were the hours spent in their room.

When they returned to Jensen, they were both very much aware that Slim only had two more operations to complete. The day after Slim returned to the base, a letter arrived with obvious American postal signs on it, addressed to Miss Jay Johnson, Jay opened it with trembling fingers, not knowing what to expect, it was obvious from the first line that Slim's mother had written it. As Jay read it, she realised that whilst thanking Jay particularly and the Johnson family in general, for the help given to Slim, she was welcoming Jay to the Nielsen family. Obviously Slim had told his family he would not marry until his operating days were over, but his mother was hoping against hope that Jay would come to *Iowa* as Slim's wife, Jay was assured of a real family welcome, the letter was signed mother. This letter gave Jay some encouragement, that if only Slim could survive the next two flights all might be well, she had been worried as to how Slim's family might view his possible marriage, now she felt a little easier.

Will and Joanne were now living at Johnsons farm, Slim had only one flight to do, it was approaching December and one night Jay counted the usual twelve planes leave the base. She was puzzled and then worried when the usual time for return passed, it was about six o'clock when she heard a plane returning, she rushed to the upper floor to sit by the window, where she had sat on so many freezing mornings, to count the returning numbers. This morning she counted only ten, two had not returned, that left the usual three hours to worry if Slim's luck had run out on his last flight. At half past nine the telephone rang it was Slim, he had survived, however he could not come to the farm until next day, four crews had completed their tour of duty and were planning to have a party that night, could Jay come at eight o'clock, of course she could, so Slim told her he would fix it with the gate. Of course all the family were pleased for Jay and particularly for Slim, the boy they had only known for six months, but whom they had taken to their hearts.

At a few minutes to eight, Jay drove up to the gate, the guard directed her to the large hut where the party was to be held, Slim was already waiting by the door. He told her the commanding officer wanted to see them, so Jay was conducted to his office by Slim, saluting the commander he remained at attention and introduced Jay, afterwards the officer gave Slim the at ease command and told them to sit down. He asked Jay about her life and if she knew that the standard of life in America might well be higher, Jay explained that her family farmed almost 1200 acres and she already had a good life, although she worked long hours. "What do you do", the officer asked,"I drive one of the tractors when there is tractor work to do", Jay told him. What about religion, the officer enquired, Jay told him she attended Jensen church as often as work would allow, it was a protestant church of England establishment. "Well at least that is a change, I see flt. Lieutenant Nielsen is also a protestant, you know most of the problems I see from this side of the desk is either, a young lady looking for an easy life in America or a protestant catholic pair and that really does give me a problem". He went on to say that he never wanted to intrude into private affairs, but he was empowered by his commanding officer, to vet likely marriages, partly to protect American officers from making a mistake and partly to protect America from camp followers and hangers on. He then went on to say that Jay must undergo a simple medical examination and Lieutenant Nielsen would make the arrangements within a few days for the camp medical team to examine her. If that is satisfactory then I will give you both my blessing willingly, with that they were both dismissed,"I think you made a good impression", Slim told Jay.

With that they returned to the party, Jay already knew Slim's crew and was soon introduced to the others, including two girls from Jensen and four from Little Staunton, who she knew anyway, there were others she did not know including a number of American nurses and women air force personnel. With the base band playing popular dance music, plenty to drink and continuous dancing, the party really went with a swing. At 10.30 the commanding officer came to the stage, calling for silence he made a patriotic speech in which he congratulated all the airmen who had now completed their tour of duty, emphasising how valuable their contribution to the war had been. Finally asking every one to stand for a minute to remember all those who would never now be able to celebrate twenty five operations successfully concluded.

After the speech the party continued and a buffet table was uncovered, holding what to Jay seemed and probably was, a banquet. Then more music and much more to drink, under camp rules the party had to finish at midnight, Jay was relieved, not being accustomed to having so much alcohol to drink and feeling quite dizzy, Slim admitted to being the same and told Jay he would come home with her. Arriving at Johnsons farm Jay opened the back door with her key and they made their way upstairs, quickly undressing they lay together quite naked. Eventually Jay began to play with the hairs on Slim's chest, he in turn, kissed and stroked Jay until neither of them could resist any longer. Slim reached for the pro-kit, then realising he had left it in his jacket he started to move towards it, Jay restrained him, "not tonight dear, I can't wait", he was told. The next morning as they lay in the half light, Slim said he was sorry if he had taken advantage of her, Jay laughing said she might have taken advantage of him, but what did it matter now, he was in no more danger and that was all Jay thought about.

Jay drove Slim to the base after breakfast, directing her to the medical unit to make an appointment for her medical check, how about 3pm this afternoon the nurse suggested, the doctor will be on duty at that time. Jay arrived early but the doctor was already present, much to Jay's surprise, a lady doctor. As she explained there were many female staff on the base and as many again on an airfield about fifteen miles away, so she covered both establishments. Telling Jay not to be worried she asked her to undress, giving her a good examination, she asked if Jay suffered from asthma, venereal disease or had any health problems and finally was she pregnant. Jay was then told to dress, that was all the doctor needed, she would submit her report to the base commander that evening. Slim met her outside and told her to collect him at six that evening. Later at Johnsons farm Slim told them he had three weeks leave and asked about first going to stay at the pub and then at the seaside again, but I must be back home a week before Christmas Jay told him, we have so many birds to pluck and many preparations for the Christmas trade.

By now Joanne was suffering morning sickness, but Jane was devoting time to her new granddaughter and this, so Joanne told her, made her feel wanted and not just suffered because she had to marry Will. Often Joanne would walk over to see her mum and Will would collect her on the BSA, although there was a resistance building up, from the older women, against Joanne riding on it. During the mornings and afternoons Joanne helped in the kitchen and although she had done very little indoor work at home she was doing very well in these household duties, but did confide to Merri that she missed driving the Fordson tractor on the farm.

During the build up to Christmas Slim decided to try his hand at plucking poultry, he had done some back home, but only turkeys for thanksgiving day. It was during a meal break in the kitchen, Slim told them he had been put under pressure to sign on for another twenty five missions, however he had refused, but agreed to help incoming crews from America to settle in and particularly help the new navigators to adapt to night flying.

Returning to the base after his leave The commanding officer told him there would be no objection to his marriage, but he should hurry it along because it was not certain how long his remaining duties in England would last, of course if he had to return to America before he was married he would not get a free passage for his wife. Urgent plans were made, Jensen church and the Rev. Williams were available on January 22nd, that just gave enough time for the banns to be read. The reception was to be held in the village hall and almost 90 guests were expected, including 20 aircrew and the commanding officer. Although it was such a rush Jay, Merri and Jane managed to produce a lovely wedding dress, with two bridesmaids dresses. Slim had the captain of Spirit of the west, as best man, but of course he was no longer piloting the aircraft, which now had a new crew. As Jay walked down the isle with Tom, her father, Slim almost took her breath away, he was so smart, not an unwanted crease, every bit of his uniform was perfect. The service went well, clear responses and hymns sung with gusto, they had been carefully chosen so both the English and American portions of the congregation were familiar with them, afterwards every one followed Slim and Mrs. Nielsen to the village hall.

Slim had provided most of the alcohol from the base but Joe had obtained a barrel of beer from the brewery and the whole family had put part of their rations towards an ample meal. After the speeches, Slim and Jay led off the dancing to the airbase band, playing the more gentle dance music at first, but soon breaking into the American style music so beloved by the young people. Before they left for their short honeymoon Slim and Jay were encouraged to lead in the Jitterbug, probably the first time the older generation had seen this American dance, soon all the younger generation were involved, particularly the aircrew. Slim and Jay slipped away to Johnsons farm to change, coming back to the reception to thank everyone for their presents and bid goodbye to the members of Slims aircrew colleagues, who were due to leave for America the next day. All the goodbyes said, Slim and Jay left in the little Austin for their honeymoon. The reception in the hall continued until almost midnight, when it finally broke up. The airmen leaving in jeeps, those that could not walk were unceremoniously thrown in the back and returned to camp, the family and villagers made unsteady progress home.

Slim and Jay sat in the bar taking a quiet, late drink before turning in, both were on familiar terms with the landlord, who insisted in sharing a drink with them to wish a happy life ahead of them. He brought himself and Slim a large whiskey and an equally large gin for Jay, afterwards climbing the stairs Jay stumbled and had to be supported by Slim, but once in the bedroom she recovered and undressed quite normally. They climbed into the high comfortable bed quite naked and lay together, Slim eventually breaking the silence, saying "at last you are Mrs. Nielsen, I am so proud of my new wife", eventually passions took over and Slim reached for the handy pro-kit, "Oh Slim not tonight, my first night as your wife surely we do not need to use that and in any case what does it matter if I do get pregnant now", for the next two days the pro-kit remained on the bedside table, untouched and unused, Jay admitted to Slim she had taken a chance but was not particularly bothered if she found out a baby was on the way.

CHAPTER SEVEN

Jay begins her new life

On the day after they returned home, Slim was told he must prepare to leave England on the 28th of January, Jay drove him to the base for the last time, there was already tension and sadness in the air, there had been tears from both Merri and Jane, even the lady working in the kitchen had moist eyes as she said goodbye to the cheerful American, Joanne had cried almost uncontrollably until Jane put her arm around her to quieten her sobs. At the airbase gate Slim and Jay climbed out of the little car, no words were said just loving arms and a passionate kiss, promises to write and a hope it would not be too long before they met again. By this time Jay was crying and Slim had to swallow hard, Jay finally said goodbye and god bless you my darling and whilst Slim watched helplessly, Jay drove home.

Jane had the kettle boiling and soon provided a cup of tea for a still tearful Jay. Eventually Jay recovered a little saying "well that is one period of my life over, I wonder what the next one holds", quietly wondering to herself if their honeymoon had left her with a baby. Jane said "if Slims family were as nice as he was then Jay must be lucky and be made to feel at home, but if she were ever in trouble and felt she must come home, Jane had enough money of her own, to pay for Jay and Slim, if necessary, to come back to Johnsons farm. Jay kissed her and told Jane she would remember, not just her kind offer but would always remember a kind and loving Grandma. Meanwhile Slim had a transfer to another airbase and slept that night, lonely and in a strange billet, thinking of Jay and wondering if he had left her with a baby, now in the cool light of day, he hoped not, feeling when Jay did have a baby, he should be there for the whole time and not leave her to be on her own. The next day Slim left England on a ferry plane taking pilots back to America who had brought new planes over the Atlantic to serve in Europe. After recovering from seeing Slim off Jay decided she could not face going out to the fields with Will so she decided to visit Jenny and particularly Margy at the garage, just before she left Merri came back from her morning lorry run, coming into Jays room and asking "Jay darling how are you now?"," sad mum, but I shall be OK now the worst is over, I have wonderful memories of our honeymoon and look forward to seeing Slim again before long", "I hope your memories are not too good, smiled Merri", "Oh maybe, but I am now Mrs. Nielsen so I suppose it does not matter too much". I keep telling myself how much more awful I should feel if I was mourning for Slim, if he had gone down over Germany, instead of us just suffering a temporary separation.

Jay set off for Little Staunton a few minutes later, it was a cold but bright day and the winter sunshine lifted her spirits a little, leaving the car on the front Jay walked into the garage and up the stairs to the Office, Jenny had gone home to prepare an early lunch for John and Margy was on her own, "Oh Jay, has Slim gone", Margy asked "yes but I am hoping it will not be too long before we meet again", Jay told her, come and sit down Margy told Jay, how was your honeymoon. "Oh wonderful, but I don't think I shall know for certain for a few days yet", "Jay you didn't do it real", "yes at least twice every day, the first night we had a few drinks and I couldn't have cared less, after that well we never bothered". Margy told Jay she was a little minx, you told me it would be dangerous, well I suppose it was, Jay said but somehow I just did not care. "Now I have something to tell you, Pat and I stopped at your reception until the end and the state of some of those American's had to be seen to be believed, but eventually we left and Pat invited me in for a drink. Well I had plenty at the reception, I knew that because I was having difficulty balancing, I have never been like that before, but we had a drink and then a kiss and before I knew it I was lying on the floor with Pat kissing me. I remember taking my dress off so it would not get damaged and Pat kissing my breasts, so I must have taken my bra off, then I can just remember an overwhelming desire to have Pat make love to me. He slid my pants off and it was wonderful, but now I am worried, mother had told me about safe periods but I never stopped to think that night". "Jay, laughed and said so we may both be in the same cart", "Oh its all right for you, with a husband it does not matter, but I am right in it if it was the wrong day, how am I going to tell mother never mind having to tell John", Margy said.

That night in the farm office Jane told them that a permit had arrived to allow them to purchase two new Fordson tractors with rubber tyres, they could of course easily afford them so perhaps a visit to the garage must be made soon to order them. Merri said she would take the permits in to Jenny, but Tom or Joe could cut the financial deal when the tractors came through. Tom asked Joe what he thought about buying a hay sweep so they could bale the hay in the field, it would save so much carting and picking, they could stack the bales under the dutch barn and build the corn into stacks. Joe thought for a moment then said why not try it, I think it might be quicker and use less labour. Talking of labour, Tom said the Seymour family are having great difficulty getting the milk ready on time, there is only one village lady they can rely on, the others have gone away to work in the factories and they are struggling to keep up with all the work on the dairy herd. I have been thinking about a milking machine, are you sure that will help Joe asked, well Fred seems to think it will help a great deal, he believes they can do all the work themselves if we buy one. It was then decided they would investigate what the purchase of a milking machine would involve.

By the end of February Jay had settled into the tractor routine, a new milking machine had been ordered to be fitted during the summer and the two new Fordson tractors were expected any day. Tom had done a deal with Jenny to take the two orange tractors in part exchange, the old Irish ones were not worth so much money and would stay on the farm. Jay had many letters from slim, she of course wrote many in return and had been able to tell him he was not yet going to be a father. Slim had been home to visit the farm for seven days and had given them an account of the wedding, his family were amazed at the wedding photographs, both how beautiful Jay was and how old and serene Jensen church had seemed.

Slims mother had written again to Jay, a long letter saying how pleased she was to look forward to welcoming an English girl to her family home, especially one as beautiful as Jay, how pleasing it was that an English family had made her son so welcome in their home. She went on to warn Jay that the weather in Iowa was not like in England, at the moment there was two feet of snow and almost twenty degrees of frost, this might carry on until well into March and in July and August there was often continuous sunshine, with the thermometer rarely below eighty degrees. Jay also received a letter from her sister in law Eliza, telling Jay how she was looking forward to having someone of her own age to talk to. The sister of Slim and Hank, Eliza's husband worked in the nearby town and did not often come home, so Eliza only had mother, there being no other house nearer than one mile, Eliza went on to say she was expecting a baby in three months time and so was finding it more difficult than usual to meet other people. Slim was now serving on the east coast but was applying for discharge to help on the family farm, partly because he was badly needed and partly so he could start rebuilding a house that needed a lot of work doing on it before he could expect Jay to live in it.

The garage in Little Staunton and the depot. on the trunk road was doing well, partly due to its country location, there being little pleasure motoring but still a heavy amount of goods traffic travelling the trunk road. Most people requiring vehicles from Little Staunton garage could, sooner or later expect to obtain a permit to buy a new lorry or tractor, whilst there were still a very few people who could get a permit for a new Anglia car. This meant there were still some new vehicles to sell and look after, also because so many old vehicles were still in use the service and spare parts side was very busy indeed. Jenny and John were working hard to help the depleted staff to cope with this volume of work, but still visited a nearby restaurant twice, sometimes three times each week, simply because they did not have time to cook a meal every night.

Margy usually ate with them, because she was now in charge of the service and parts accounts and just as busy as everyone else. John and Margy were very close, Margy had adopted him as the father she had never known, John was proud of this and devoted to her. David was always civil and would have a laugh with John but was never as close to him as Margy, probably because he lived away most of the time. Margy, now twenty three years old, sat with John and Jenny in the house after one of these visits to the restaurant. Margy asked her mother if she remembered telling her she was thinking of marrying John,"of course", Jenny told her "and do you remember what I said. That why should you risk having another baby at your time of life, you replied you thought that could be avoided, well you avoided it quite well, but I have not done so". They both looked at her startled, "you mean you are pregnant" Jenny asked, "fraid so mum, I am sorry but cannot do anything about it now".

Jenny asked who the father was, "Oh Pat of course, I have never been out with anyone else", Jenny asked how it happened, she told Margy that she had thought she had given her all the information she thought her daughter needed to avoid this situation. "Oh you did mother, but it did not take into account Jays wedding the drinks and emotions of that night, you remember I came home with Pat, but his parents were away that night and he invited me in for a last drink. Margy told them Pat was as happy as Margy was and before she knew it, she was demanding that Pat make love to her, the rest they could imagine. Jenny asked if Pat knew, Margy told them she had not told him yet, but he was due on leave for two weeks this weekend and Margy intended to tell him then. John moved over to Margy asking if she really wanted to marry Pat, because if she had any doubts she must not do so, he would support her if need be. But Margy told them she loved Pat and was only sorry that her moment of carelessness had caused such a problem. Jenny said it was not a problem if Pat loved Margy enough to marry her, because Jenny had respected Pat's devotion to the garage before he was called up and she had already thought he would make a good replacement for Bertie when he retired. Jay received a letter from Slim to say his discharge was expected any day, he had been told that American brides left in England for three months could expect shipping documents soon. Jay ,was of course, overjoyed, but sad at the same time, believing it would be many years before she saw her family again. Joe had decided Jay should have a British passport before she was married and this had been obtained. Joe was now seventy five years old and Jay, without mentioning it, felt she would never see either her grandfather or grandmother again after she had left for her new life in America.

Joanne was now becoming visibly pregnant and now, as Jay knew, Margy was also having a baby. Jay had been present at the wedding, held in Staunton register office, with the reception at Johnsons farm. The Graham's, Margy's grandparents, and brother David were present, as was Pats family, it was rather a subdued affair, but nevertheless, because Pat and Margy were obviously in love, it had an overall sense of happiness. In May, just before the war finished in Europe, Jay received a bulky envelope from the American embassy, it was a large guide to America an outline of American customs and practices, plus a ticket, second class, for a single journey on a passenger liner, leaving Liverpool in two weeks time.

Jay wrote to Slim, telling him the date she was due in New York, but he must have already had the details, because the next day a letter arrived, telling Jay he would be there to meet her. Now there was such a rush, Jay had to decide what she wanted to take with her, after much thought, packing and re-packing, she decided on two pairs of overalls, all her underwear, and a selection of everyday clothes, plus one best dress, she bought small presents for Slims family and finally fastened down her case. Just before she left, the momentous news came that Germany had surrendered, the VE celebrations, unleashed a frenzy of cheering and shouting, plus not a little drinking, but Jays heart was already with Slim in America. The day Jay left was really heart breaking, even saying goodbye to the faithful little Austin, brought a lump to her throat, she had finally given it to Will and Joanne. Jay had said her goodbyes to the Garage staff and the Simpsons the previous day, not without a few tears it may be said. But the morning she left the farm all the staff assembled to say goodbye, there were more tears but quite a few smiles, wishes of well being and promises to write. Joe and Jane hugged her particularly long and hard, both no doubt aware that it was unlikely they would ever see her again, even Joe shed a few tears before Tom and Merri drove her to the station. Luckily the train was on time, so the wait was not long, but even so a few more tears were shed.

A girl with mixed feeling arrived in Liverpool, sad to leave England but so looking forward to seeing Slim again. She took a taxi to the embarkation pier as directed on her instructions and after what seemed an interminable wait, was shown to a cabin with four bunks in the second class part of the ship. Her ticket specified the number of her berth as six B, so stowing her case in the place allocated to it, she threw her nightgown and toilet bag on to the bunk.

181

Leaving the cabin Jay went to explore the ship, soon finding a barrier with a notice,"no second class passengers beyond this point". Nevertheless Jay was impressed by the size of the ship and its cafe's and restaurant, also its dance floor. Returning to her cabin she found another girl had arrived. Introducing herself as Jacky, whilst they were talking yet another passenger was shown in. This was Carol and obviously pregnant, eventually, they ran upstairs to find the ship moving out into the river Mersey. Standing on deck they could see the lights of Liverpool shining, no blackout now, but there were many blank spaces where no lights shone, a memorial to the blitz. The Royal Liver building with its twin towers could just be seen in the near darkness, eventually after watching their homeland disappear and full of emotion, Jacky said " come on I am hungry, they took dinner in the restaurant and after a trip to the dance hall, which was almost empty, they retired to bed.

With Jay gone Johnsons farm was rather subdued for a day or so, but work had to go on, the hay harvest was almost upon them yet again. A tractor driver had to be found to take the place of Jay, this was solved by Will working full time on one tractor and a borrowed boy, from the garage, not yet old enough to go into the forces, driving the other one. In the middle of June Joanne gave birth, with the assistance of Jane, to a boy, Thomas Joseph Johnson, Joanne deciding she could take over one of the tractors in the middle of August, accompanying her husband Will in the fields. Jane again becoming nursemaid full time, Merri working in the kitchen, along with the village lady and doing the lorry deliveries at each end of the day. The milking machine was being fitted, a silver pipeline from one end of the shed to the other, over each run of cows heads, with a tap for each standing of two cows, to which a bucket and cluster of teat cups could be connected, was soon fitted. The dairy was altered to accommodate six buckets and teat cup clusters, both for cleaning and storing, with an electric motor driving a vacuum pump the installation was complete. After some initial difficulties with accustoming the cows to the new and frightening operation, it all settled down and was found that Fred and Adrian Seymour could milk all the cows by themselves, it was greeted as a step forward into the twentieth century. The hay sweep was found to speed up the hay harvest, it was necessary to let the hay ripen a little longer in the field, but additional turning helped to cut down this time, and once it was ready, a tractor pushing great sweep fulls of hay to the baler, driven by the W30 tractor, made speedy work of making the crop safe from any inclement weather that may come along. The bales made into a simple stack could be carted at any time it was convenient, over the next few weeks. The corn harvest came along all too quickly, but although the prisoner gangs were no longer available, a gang of land girls replaced them, although other farms in the district had used them in the past and found them very willing, but unskilled, those that came to Johnsons farm worked hard and were a great assistance.

Billy no longer built the stacks, it was now beyond his strength, but his son Jacky had taken to that job and it must be said made some very respectable stacks. Walter and Jim picked sheaves in the field and Tom loaded the waggons. Two land girls helped Jacky on the stack and one unloaded the sheaves on to the elevator, this was hard work and so another land girl tidied up the stackyard and took turns to unload, one other girl ferried the waggons field and farm. Tom was already getting interested in a combine harvester, but had decided to wait a while yet until he had seen one at work and assessed just how much it may help with the labour shortage. After the corn harvest the five land girls were offered the chance to stay in the unoccupied rooms in the farmhouse and harvest the root crops, this they accepted and so the kitchen work increased but Elsie and Merri coped quite well, so the autumn work on Johnsons farm seemed to be under control, at least labour wise.

After dinner on the boat the three girls retired to bed, none of them knew if they were good sailors but by now they were committed, as Jay said, it could only be for a few days anyway and they might have a smooth crossing. The first day out was very still and smooth, then for two days the boat rolled, but they were OK, but on the fourth day and the beginning of the fifth it was really rough. Poor Carol suffered badly but Jay and Jacky, although feeling a little off colour, were not sick, but none of them ate any dinner. Eventually the motion of the boat eased and they went on deck, there was an amazing sight, the statue of liberty, not too far away and the tremendous skyline of New York behind it. The usual muddle of disembarking, but after two and a half hour Jay cleared immigration and ran into Slims arms. Jay had become separated from her companions, but who cared, she had a smiling Slim again. Slim had been discharged nearly a week ago, but had managed to stay on camp until yesterday, when he had come to meet Jay, staying in New York for the last evening.

Slim picked up Jay's case and they took a cab to the central station, Jay was fascinated with the city, its lights, mass of traffic and the tall towering buildings and of course the unbelievable mass of people. It was at central station that Jay realised how hungry she was, not having any food for nearly two days, by the time they had eaten and Slim had reclaimed his luggage from the left luggage office it was time to board the train, the porter showed them to their sleeping cabin and they fell into one anothers arms. They soon lay together on the bunk, Slim locked the door, after a few minutes, whilst Jay took off her dress, a smiling Slim told her he hoped she was going to take off more than just her dress, Jay replying she hoped Slim was going to take off the rest of her clothes. Slim with many affectionate kisses, gently removed Jay's clothes, until she was totally naked, Slim by this time was also in that state. They lay together, holding one another and gently kissing, eventually Jay told Slim he just had to love her properly, she could wait no longer, but whispered it should be safe tonight. They did not notice the train move off, for a long time, but eventually Jay decided they must get dressed and see what was going on outside. It was dark, New York was behind them but there were many lights still moving past, " will I see your family tomorrow ", Jay asked, "no the next day" Slim told her, Jay was surprised, asking how far it was, Slim replied that he thought it about one thousand miles, perhaps a bit more. They had a rather elegant dinner in the dining car and retired to bed, to celebrate their reunion all over again.

Another day and another night followed, Jay was just struck dumb by the sheer size of her new country and fascinated by the different crops and small towns she saw as the train continued to roll onwards. On the second day the train stopped at mid morning and they climbed down on to the platform, Slim pointed out his family, running towards them,

185

Jay just had time to see his father, white haired but straight backed, a rather plump, but not fat lady and an older version of Slim accompanied by a dark girl obviously pregnant and a clean cut girl, sister Jan. Slim introduced them all, each gave Jay a kiss and a handshake, but Slims mum whispered "you are even lovelier than your photograph and thank you for looking after Slim so well. Jan was the first to move, saying she must get back to work, but would see Jay at the weekend. Walking into a rather dusty street Jay saw a large car parked and Slims father walking over to it, hank and his wife climbed into the front seat whilst Slim, Jay and mother sat in the back. A bit different to the old Austin eh Slim remarked, Jay reminded him with a smile, he had been pleased enough to ride in it, as Jay remembered.

"Well Ma. what do you think to her", Slim asked, "I think she is lovely and what a nice way of talking she has", mother replied, smiling at Jay as she said it. Jay asked how far it was to the farm,"Oh about thirty miles I guess", father told her, the country had already opened out and Jay could see crops she had never seen before. Eventually they turned off the tarmac road and about a half mile further on, they turned into a smaller road, leading to a large yard with a long two story house facing, a wonderful large barn overshadowing the house on its right hand side, with the top of another building plainly in view above the house roof. Between the two barns and looking fairly new was a much smaller house, whilst on the left hand side of the main house was another house obviously undergoing renovation. Welcome to your new home Slim said, that one on the left will be ours when I have finished it, Slim, mother instructed, bring those cases in, this girl must be worn out, what a journey you have had honey, just follow me and we will have a cool drink. Jay was soon sitting in a large kitchen, with a scrubbed table and a glass of lemonade in her hand, Slim came into the kitchen. He said "I guess honey, you can now see why I felt so at home in Johnsons farm kitchen.", " yes there is so much that is similar", Jay replied, they sat talking for a while and eventually Hank and Eliza left to walk home, leaving mother, father and Slim sitting together. Mother said "I will prepare dinner, I left it all ready this morning". While she busied herself with dinner, Slim asked Jay if she felt up to a walk round the farm. Walking out the door they turned into the front barn, to Jay it was immense, it held two John Deere tractors, an International W30 also a lorry, whilst behind these was a collection of arable implements and a combine harvester. Slim informed her the combine was new last year and had been bought to ease the labour problem whilst Slim was away. As they passed Hank's house, Eliza called from the door "Jay honey, come round in the morning for coffee", "thank you about ten then" Jay replied.

The second barn was partitioned by a large stout fence, Slim explained they usually ran fifty steers on the farm, apart from the one thousand acres of wheat, three hundred acres of corm (maize), there was four hundred acres of woodland and three hundred acres of grassland. The second barn housed the steers in the winter and provided both good growth for the steers and a large quantity of manure. Behind the barn, unseen by Jay until that moment was a long low stack of hay bales and two grain silos. Finally Slim told her "come and see our house", walking in through the door Jay was met by a wonderful smell of pine, Slim had panelled the kitchen and parlour in pine, giving the place this wonderful smell. In the kitchen Slim proudly showed her a refrigerator and a washing machine, "we are lucky to be connected to the mains electricity", Slim told her, going on to say, that many farms still use kerosene or have a generator. Upstairs, still in need of decorating but dry and sound were three rooms and a bathroom. Slim had decided they could move in when the bathroom and front bedroom were decorated, but would have to wait for the payout from the harvest before he could afford to buy furniture for the other rooms. "Oh Slim what a lovely big house and its all made of wood", well yes he told her almost all the houses are made of wood out west, there is such a good supply and our house, although not used for a long time is still sound and dry and will be warm in the winter. Returning to the kitchen, the dinner was almost ready and they were soon sitting round the table eating a delicious meal, Slim looking at Jay said "now you know how I appreciated Johnsons farm home baking, after the air force meals.

Clearing away the dinner things, mother prepared the coffee and then mother and Jay washed up. Sitting around the table with the coffee, they talked about the farm, father (pop) telling Jay how his grandfather had come as a young man to start the farm after his emigration, with a young wife, from Norway. Jay told them the story of Johnsons farm and how it had evolved over the years. Ma. then said time for bed, Jay gratefully took the hint and climbed the stairs with Slim to their bedroom. The next morning Pop suggested Jay and Slim should try to make their house habitable, he reckoned a week to ten days and the harvest would start and then there would be no time for anything but fieldwork. Jay cleaned and scrubbed the the parlour whilst Slim did the wiring and plumbing in the kitchen, at a few minutes to ten Jay reminded him she must go to see Eliza and would then call on Ma. to see if she could do anything for her. Eliza was ready with the coffee pot and some small home made cakes, they chatted together, Eliza telling Jay her baby was due in four weeks time, but she was suffering from the heat. "For goodness sake try and start a baby in late spring and avoid all this terrible heat", Eliza told her. Jay told Eliza they did not plan to start a family until the house was finished, but then, as Jay said, one never knows. Jay feeling happy with her visit to Eliza called on Ma. to see if she could help with anything, "goodness no child, I can manage a simple meal, you go and help Slim". Four days later the kitchen was finished except for a table and chairs, the parlour almost complete and the bedroom decorated. Ma. suggested they use the bed and wardrobe from Slims room and use an old table and two chairs from an outhouse until they had money to buy new ones, so they had a house of their own and before the harvest started.

Slim could now concentrate on preparing for the harvest by helping Hank and Pop. One day, just before the harvest started Slim told Jay they must go and cut some wood for the kitchen stove, or goodness only knows when we shall have time again he said, off they went to the wood taking lunch with them, it was so interesting to Jay, she had never been involved in this kind of work before. They cut down mostly pine trees, trimming the brash away and then cutting the trunk into log lengths for the kitchen stove, which also cooked the food and provided a simple large bore central heating system. That night as they lay in the warm air of their bedroom Slim began to show his desire for Jay, she of

189

course responded. But tonight told Slim he must usa a pro-kit, it was not the time to take chances, but nevertheless they made leisurely and satisfying love, Slim smiling at Jay asked when she might be ready to start a family. Jay told him she expected to be ready in the spring, so she was not too big and hot in the summer sun, but could look forward to a cool winter baby. "I can see you have it all planned", Slim said, he agreed and the subject was left at that.

Two days later the combine harvester was driven out of the barn and into the first field of wheat, at dinner that night Pop said he was surprised that no casual worker had called to see if he could help in the harvest. Because the first six hundred acres of wheat had been sold it had to be delivered to the silo, about five miles away. This meant that with Pop driving the combine, Slim driving the lorry and Hank a tractor and trailer the combine had to keep waiting for an empty vehicle to return from the silo, Pop thought an extra hand to drive another tractor and trailer would keep the combine going full time.

Jay looked at Pop, saying she had realised that, having ridden in the lorry with Slim and was about to propose she drove the third unit. Why on earth did they need another hand, after all she told them, I have been driving tractors since I left school. Pop looked at Jay, asking if she was sure she could handle one of their tractors,"of course, we have a W30 back home to drive our threshing set, often when it has not been threshing I have driven it on the land", Jay told him. "You know Pop. am so interested in your way of farming, so different to ours, your combine enthrals me, but it may not work so well in England, our straw is so long and our crops so much heavier than yours. Pop asked how much wheat they might get to an acre, Jay told him about two and a half tons, in an exceptional crop it may be up to three tons. Gee, Pop told her, "a good crop here may be up to one and a half tons to an acre, the crop we have been harvesting today is just less than that". "I notice your combine spreads the straw, so I suppose you then plough it in", Jay said. "Yes, but when we work closer to the buildings we shall leave some straw in rows so we can bale it for winter bedding for the beef stock". Pop asked if they still used a binder back home, Jay laughed, telling him they did, but going on to say,"hey Pop this is my home now".

"you really think you could handle a tractor and trailer to the silo", Pop asked,"sure I could and I know the way now and to be sure and get a ticket from the weighbridge", Jay told him. The next morning, whilst Pop and Hank started off the combine, Slim and Jay hitched the W30 tractor to a high sided trailer and set off for the field. Hank had almost a trailer full and after one more tankful of grain was added to his trailer he set off for the silo. Jay soon followed, "take it slow this first load", Slim told her. She met Hank on his way back and they passed with a smile and a wave, as she approached the farm, Slim passed with his lorry loaded and as she entered the combine plot Hank was almost full.

So that was how they spent the day, during dinner Pop reckoned up the silo weigh tickets and said they had delivered seventy tons of wheat, that was a real good day he said. Eliza, now getting close to having her baby had been helping Mom, as she called her, in the kitchen so both Eliza and Hank stayed to dinner. Eventually after much talk and when the coffee pot was empty, the ladies washed up the dinner pots and the two families departed to their homes. Jay and Slim, both tired, but particularly Jay, decided they must have a shower before bed. Jay soon stood naked, entering the shower she found a smiling Slim follow her in, he proceeded to soap her and soon had himself and Jay thoroughly aroused. Not stopping to rinse off the soap they joined lips and whilst Slim explored her mouth with his tongue, Jay did likewise, the water ran down their faces and over their bodies. After a few minutes of this wonderful experience, Slim placed his hands under Jay's buttocks and raised her up, Jay, almost by instinct put her legs round Slim's waist whilst the water still ran over them. A further kiss or two and Jay was conscious of Slim's need, as he touched her most sensitive and private parts, Jay wriggled down and believed he was almost entering her. Then she did a quite spontaneous thing, on the spur of the moment, Jay leaned back, holding herself by locking her hands behind Slim's neck. Slim pulled her tighter to him and Jay felt a wonderful sensation as Slim slipped further, and with a little more wriggling, further than ever inside Jay. There they stayed for perhaps two or three minutes, with just the occasional wriggle, until Jays back could stand it no longer and she pulled herself close to Slim's face, kissing him with considerable feeling. Jay knew instinctively Slim had slipped out of the wonderful place he had been, Jay moved her legs from round his waist and stood before him. Standing close together with the water pouring over them, they held one another saying nothing for a short time, then Slim turned off the water and handed Jay a towel. Afterwards, lying in bed together, Jay smiled at him, saying she was not very certain they should have behaved as they had in the shower. I thought it was safe to make love now, Slim told her, we have been using contraceptives for five days, maybe it is, but it felt so different, Jay told him, you may have lost your spare tractor driver for the spring work.

A week later and all the wheat that was destined for the grain company was delivered and the four hundred acres due to be stored on the farm was started, now three carting units were not needed to keep the combine in full operation, two units only could handle the job. Pop asked Jay if she still wanted to work on the farm,"of course", she told him so Pop suggested she start and disc harrow the wheat ground, to stop the weeds growing and help to make the straw easier to bury when it was ploughed, so Jay had a new job. She worked from eight till eight, as the combine did, taking sandwiches and two bottles of mom's lemonade with her. After three days Slim came running across to her, telling he Hank had to take Eliza to the hospital, would Jay come and help cart the grain to the farm.

Because Jay was available to carry grain, there was no urgency for Hank to start work quickly, but he came home to take dinner with them, saying Eliza was in labour and he would soon return to the hospital. At breakfast the next morning, a happy Hank was able to tell them that Eliza had a baby girl and could Jay drive the tractor to-day so he could return to the hospital. In fact Jay drove the tractor for a week until Eliza was back home with her daughter and again up and about. By this time it was August and although the wheat was finished the corn (maize) would not be ready for some time, Jay and Slim worked on the wheat ground whilst Pop and Hank baled the straw and carted it into the barn. Jay, much to her relief, had proved not to be having a baby after the adventure in the shower and she had warned Slim they really must be more careful, Slim professed to be pleased, but Jay thought perhaps she could detect just a trace of disappointment. Eliza was now able to help Mom in the kitchen, when she was not feeding and looking after her daughter, Brigit, so the whole family still took dinner together at night. Jay of course, lost no time in visiting Eliza when she returned from hospital, the two girls, of similar age, were good friends and confidants, Jay telling Eliza of the shower episode.

When Jan came at the weekend she was soon told of Jay's escapade, she laughed, telling them she just knew how Jay felt, but thought those kinds of adventures were not for her. Jay had finished disc harrowing the wheat ground whilst Pop and Hank put on the corn headers to the combine, only one trailer was required to carry the corn to the farm corn silo. So Slim and Jay therefore were left with one thousand acres of wheat land to plough, they started this during August, they had been married eight months.

The weather became hot and humid, one lunch time as they sat together in the shade of a large tree on the edge of the wood, eating their packed lunch together, Jay suddenly said, I must take off my bra. I am so hot. She unfastened the shoulder straps of her overalls and took off her shirt, turning to Slim she asked him to undo the clips on her bra, Slim soon had the clips undone, but before Jay could slip on her shirt, Slim turned her towards him and started to kiss her, Jay responded quite quickly. Easing her down on to the warm dry grass he began to kiss her neck and followed this by tracing the wonderful valley between her breasts with his tongue, then tantalisingly used his tongue to tickle the nipples on her breasts. Easing her up he slipped her overalls out of the way and continued to kiss her flat stomach and her thighs, by now Jay was very much aroused. As Slim eased her up again to slip off her pants, Jay managed to collect herself together enough to say "no not today without protection", "well I don't have a pro-kit

194

here, Slim told her, letting her down on the ground with her pants still in place.

Slim took off his shirt and trousers, saying never mind we will just play for a little while, Jay watched this operation with a smile on her lips. As Slim again turned to her he kissed her face, continued kissing her lips and breasts, then lying together for some time just kissing, with Slim stroking her thighs. Jay lay perfectly still, just touching Slim, but being very much aware he was aroused, Jay could feel her breasts so hard she had the feeling they would burst. Slim kissed her lips again, exploring her mouth and still gently massaging the inside of her thighs. Jay realised she had unconsciously opened her legs wide, as Slim broke away from her lips for a moment she whispered,"take off my pants darling", Jay eased up and Slim quickly slid them off, when this was done he again kissed her. With one arm under her neck Slim, so very gently teased the nipple of a hard and willing breast, Jay opened her legs again and Slim just naturally slipped inside her. As he gently moved inside Jay, she could feel all caution leaving her body, all she now wanted was Slim, all of him. He eventually started slowly to withdraw, but before this was completed Jay lifted her head, put her arms around his neck and gave him a most passionate kiss, Slim immediately responded and started to move inside her again. Jay knew deep inside herself she must not let him do this, especially to-day, but her demands far outstripped her caution and Jay continued to encourage him to make real love to her.

Eventually they lay together in a state of semi exhaustion, after some time Jay looked at him with a smile, all that because I wanted to take off my bra. "Ah but was that all", Slim asked, well I think I knew we should not stop, indeed

I think I knew all morning that you must love me at midday, even though I knew it was most dangerous to do. I had decided not to tempt you but when we sat together I decided to take off my bra and see where it led us and how lovely it was, but I hope we still think so next May.

EPILOGUE

Johnsons farm had a good harvest that year and the farm was prosperous, Will and Joanne had a son in August, and Margy had a daughter in September, Jenny and John were entranced with her whilst Pat and Margy were so happy. Margy still worked in the office with baby Jennifer (Jen) with her, Pat would come upstairs on almost any pretence to see his daughter. Joanne on Johnsons farm, took over one tractor whilst her son, by tradition, was looked after in the farm kitchen and nursery. Will drove the second tractor but by spring of the next year Joe became ill and eventually died. The whole family was affected, Joe had seemed the rock on which the family fortune was built and his loss was felt very deeply. Tom remembering how Joe had taught him so well, soon made Will aware of his responsibilities and took him away from the tractor, so they could spend the time together, that Tom had spent with Joe. As they looked for another tractor driver to replace Will, Joanne suggested they should look for two, she believed she had started a baby about the time of Joe's death.

In America Jay knew she and Slim were to become parents in the next May, never mind, Jay said I shall be able to help in the harvest to carry the wheat, Eliza has said she will look after the baby. Jay had settled well in America, having very little home sickness, she even escaped most of the morning sickness that had so troubled Eliza. Many were the letters that flowed between Jay and her family in England, Jay felt that Merri was giving her all the news and Jay could still almost see the farm and Jensen village.

The sad letter carrying the news of Joe's death really devastated Jay, probably more so because she was now so big, mom and Pop would not let her work and so she had time to think. After the funeral day had passed she felt a little better and the news that Will and Joanne were expecting another baby, she thought, helped her. Then one day she made her usual morning coffee call on Eliza, only to find her looking ill and almost in tears, whatever is the matter Jay asked. I'm pregnant again, Jay was told and Hank promised he would look after me, but he took advantage of me two months ago, he let me down and now I shall have to go through all that again. "Oh Eliza it takes two to make a deal, look how I got caught, are you sure it is not just a bit your fault", "well I did encourage him a bit I suppose". Later in the spring Jay gave birth to a boy, John, the family came to see a happy and contented Jay in hospital and later she helped with the harvest just as she had planned, Eliza looked after John but would Jay enjoy the Autumn cultivations as much this year as last. Will we ever learn more about Johnsons farm and Jay's life in America, probably not, but who knows what the future may bring.